'You've chan[ged], Rachel,' he said[.]

'Oh, dear,' she said, 'that sounds ominous. Although I suppose it's inevitable, really, after all this time, that one would look older…'

'I wasn't talking about looking older.'

'Well, I'm sorry I'm no longer pretty,' she said with a short laugh.

'You're beautiful,' he said softly, and suddenly she realised he was right behind her, so close that if she moved as much as an inch they would be touching. She froze.

'Your hair,' he went on, 'it's lovely. You used to wear it shorter, but I like it long like that.'

She sensed rather than saw him reach out his hand, then was aware that he was touching her hair. This wasn't happening, she told herself; she couldn't let this happen—it had taken her months, no, years to get over him the last time, if she ever had. She simply couldn't let it happen again. She moved away from him on the pretext of taking the sugar bowl from the cupboard above the worktops. Stretching up, she opened the cupboard doors, and it was then that she felt his arms go round her.

THE POLICE DOCTOR'S DISCOVERY

BY
LAURA MacDONALD

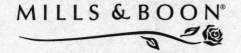

MILLS & BOON®

*All the characters in this book have no existence outside the imagination
of the author, and have no relation whatsoever to anyone bearing the
same name or names. They are not even distantly inspired by any
individual known or unknown to the author, and all the incidents are
pure invention.*

*First published in Great Britain 2004
Harlequin Mills & Boon Limited,
Eton House, 18-24 Paradise Road, Richmond, Surrey TW9 1SR*

© Laura MacDonald 2004

ISBN 0 263 83938 9

*Set in Times Roman 10½ on 12 pt.
03-1204-49978*

*Printed and bound in Spain
by Litografia Rosés, S.A., Barcelona*

CHAPTER ONE

'NICK!' She stopped dead as the main doors of Westhampstead Police Headquarters closed behind her and the dark-haired man talking to the desk sergeant turned to face her.

'Rachel…?' There was a flash of something in his eyes along with recognition—shock? Pleasure maybe? She wasn't sure, she only knew that her heart had turned over at the sight of him and even now was hammering uncomfortably in her chest. 'What are you doing here?' The eyes as dark as his hair narrowed slightly.

'I could ask you the same question.' She managed to speak lightly, even though her heart continued to perform gymnastics at the sudden and unexpected sight of this man who had once meant so much to her.

'I work here,' he said simply, 'or didn't you know?'

'I knew you were a policeman certainly, but I thought you were with the Metropolitan Police.'

'I was,' he said, 'but I've recently transferred back here to Westhampstead.'

'So we've both come home.'

'You've returned?'

'For the time being, yes.' She swallowed, still struggling to control her reactions. 'One of the partners at the group practice is taking a year's sabbatical—I'm filling in for him.'

'So how can we help you?'

'Dr Beresford.' The voice of the duty sergeant broke in and Nick Kowalski turned slightly towards the man, whom to Rachel's relief seemed to know exactly who she was and why she was there. He extended his hand and enclosed hers in a huge paw-like grip. 'I'm station sergeant—Harry Mason.'

'I thought I'd come and familiarise myself with the place before I'm called out,' said Rachel, aware that beside her Nick had grown very still.

'Called out?' He frowned and just for a moment Rachel was glad that she had this slight advantage over him.

'Yes,' she said smoothly, 'I'm to provide medical cover for this station.'

'I thought that was Steve O'Malley's job,' said Nick and Rachel thought she detected a sudden sharp edge to his voice, almost as if greeting her and talking to her were one thing but having her work there was another thing altogether.

'It's Steve who's on sabbatical,' she replied calmly. 'Like I said, I'm taking his place.'

'Have you done any police work before?' It was almost an accusation and Rachel saw a frown cross Harry Mason's face.

'As it happens, yes, I have.' She spoke coolly, in control now. 'I was Police Doctor at my last practice in Stockport.'

'Let me show you around.' As if he sensed some sort of tension between the two of them, Harry Mason beckoned to a young constable to take over the desk.

But Nick interjected before the constable had time to move. 'I'll do that, Harry,' he said curtly. Glancing at Rachel, he added, 'If you have no objections?'

'Well, no.' She hesitated slightly, aware that Harry Mason seemed put out at having his role hijacked but at the same time suspecting that Nick Kowalski was pulling rank. 'Of course not.' She had no idea of Nick's rank, as he was not in uniform, but as she followed him down the corridor she found her thoughts in turmoil. She'd known he'd gone into the police force, of course she had. Hadn't there been conjecture at the time that Westhampstead's wild boy might turn to enforcing the law instead of ending up behind bars, as so many had predicted he would?

Her suspicions of his high rank intensified as they passed a man in the corridor, also in plain clothes, who nodded at Nick and muttered the single word, 'Guv.'

'You're CID?' she asked as he led the way past a huge control room and opened the door of an office, standing back for her to precede him.

'Yes.' He nodded.

'Rank?' she asked as he closed the door behind them. 'DCI.'

'I'm impressed,' she said softly. 'Detective Chief Inspector—who would have thought it?'

'Who indeed?' His gaze met hers levelly. 'Certainly not the good folk of Westhampstead, that's for sure.'

'You've done well, Nick.' She glanced around the office as she spoke, at the desk, the filing cabinets, the computer and phones—anywhere rather than at the dark gaze that was still levelled at her with that same, albeit slight measure of accusation, as if for all those years he'd carried the assumption that she and her family, and indeed many others in their home town, had believed he would never amount to much.

'Yes, well.' He shrugged, then, his eyes narrowing again, he added, 'You haven't done so bad yourself, Rachel—but, then, I don't think there was ever any doubt that you would.' He paused but his comments were loaded and for a moment, as once again her gaze was dragged back to his own, they were both transported back to their youth and the anguish of the love they had shared.

'So.' It was Nick who recovered first, apparently pulling himself together and turning his head away from her so that she couldn't see the pain that had flared in his eyes. 'Do you think you might stay in Westhampstead this time?'

'I don't know.' She shook her head. 'Steve has only gone for a year—but if I like it here there may be an opening at the practice when Calvin Davenport, the senior partner, retires. So, who knows? I may just decide to stay.'

'Where are you living—with your parents?' Did his lip curl ever so slightly at mention of her parents, or had she imagined it?

'No, at a house in Cathedral Close.'

'Very cosy.' He raised his eyebrows and she thought she detected a faintly mocking air about him now. It irritated her and drove her to retaliate.

'And you?' she said. 'I heard you were married—I dare say by now you have a horde of children.'

'I have one daughter,' he said quietly, and Rachel felt a sudden sharp stab of some emotion she was unable to define. 'And my marriage ended in divorce.'

Rachel wished she hadn't spoken. 'I'm sorry,' she muttered.

'It's OK.' He shrugged. 'Unfortunately marriage and my career weren't compatible.'

'Do you see your daughter?'

'Yes, she lives with her mother but she visits me whenever the job allows me the time.' He paused. 'And you, Rachel—are you married?' The tension in the small room seemed heightened as he waited for her reply.

'No.' She shook her head. 'I'm in a long-term relationship…'

'And?'

'I felt it wasn't going anywhere so this year is by way of a decider…' She trailed off. 'I don't know why I'm telling you this.' She gave a quick, dismissive gesture.

He grinned and for a moment the tension between them dissolved and he was once again the Nick Kowalski she had once known—the wild boy from the wrong side of town, the boy with a motorbike who had only kept out of trouble with the law by not being caught, the boy with laughter in his wicked black eyes, the boy deemed wholly unsuitable for Rachel Beresford, only daughter of Westhampstead's highly respected GP and his wife, Diana, herself a magistrate.

'Come on,' he said, 'let me show you around and introduce you to the rest of the crew. I'm sure you'll find them a good bunch on the whole.'

'I'm sure I shall,' said Rachel as she followed him out of his office and into the control room.

Half an hour later Rachel found herself sitting in her car in the car park of police headquarters. Before switching on the ignition, she sat for a while, her hands resting on the steering-wheel as she gazed up at the building before her. It had been a shock seeing Nick again, she couldn't deny that. Even though since her return to Westhampstead she had met up with many old friends and acquaintances, she hadn't expected to see Nick because she hadn't known that he, too, had returned to their home town.

For a moment it had taken her right back to that long hot summer when she had returned from her girls' boarding school for the holidays and had taken the car her parents had given her for passing her exams into the garage where Nick had worked as a mechanic. She'd seen him before, of course, around the town when she had been at home on holiday, and had long been attracted to his dark good looks and the stories of his rather wild reputation, but it had been that visit to the garage that had been the start of their brief, passionate affair. He'd asked her out and had picked her up from home on his motorbike, roaring off into the night with her riding pillion. Her parents had been appalled and had done everything in their power to bring the romance to an end. But Rachel had fallen head over heels in love and had had no intention of giving up her new boyfriend. They had spent the whole of that long hot summer together and when at last Rachel had gone to medical school she and Nick had written to each other for weeks.

But then his letters had suddenly stopped, leaving Rachel hurt and bewildered, and shortly afterwards Rachel's mother had told her that she had seen Nick in town with someone else. Several years later Rachel had heard that he had married another local girl, the daughter of a friend of his mother. She in turn had got on with her own life and had thought she had put the boy from the wrong side of town firmly out of her mind.

Seeing him today had shown her otherwise and had brought the past sharply into focus once more. She wondered if he, too, had felt as she had, but somehow she doubted it. After all, it had been Nick who had stopped the contact between them, Nick who had married someone else. Not that she had carried a torch for him all these years, she told herself firmly. After all, she'd had Jeremy, hadn't she? She frowned at the thought of Jeremy and at the way their relationship had gone, then with a little sigh she started the engine and drove out of the car park.

The Beresford Medical Centre, named after its foun-
der, Rachel's father James, was situated in an old
Victorian house in a leafy avenue in the fashionable part
of Westhampstead. James Beresford had retired some
years previously and together with his wife was still living in Ashton House, the family home on the far side of
town where Rachel had been brought up. Rachel's
mother was in poor health, having recently been diag-
nosed with Alzheimer's disease, and both she and her
husband had been delighted when Rachel had agreed to
take up the position at the medical centre.

'It's what we've always wanted,' her father had said
as he'd hugged her.

'I know,' Rachel had replied, 'but you mustn't forget
this is only a trial run—it may not turn out to be what
I want permanently.'

'Perhaps Jeremy will want to move down here,' her
father had added hopefully.

'I shouldn't count on it,' Rachel had replied.

Now, as she entered the large hallway of the house,
which had been turned into a spacious reception area,
she made a conscious effort to put Jeremy out of her
mind and concentrate on the fact that she would have a
full afternoon surgery to face. But as she collected the
bundle of patient records that receptionist Danielle
Quilter passed to her, she found, somewhat disconcert-
ingly, that it wasn't Jeremy who dogged her thoughts
but Nick.

'Are you OK, Rachel?' asked Danielle, peering up
into her face.

'Yes.' Rachel paused and frowned. 'Why?'

'You look pale,' said the girl, 'like you've just seen
a ghost.'

Rachel blinked. 'Like I've just…?' she said, then she

gave a short laugh. 'Ha! Well, maybe I have.' Shaking her head, she made her way up the stairs and down a short corridor to the large first-floor room that was Steve O'Malley's consulting room and which had been allocated to her for her time at the centre.

The room, at the rear of the house, with its huge sash windows, overlooked the garden, which was enclosed by a high, red-brick wall. Now, as September got into its stride, the leaves on the trees were turning gold and the herbaceous borders, which through the summer months had been a blaze of colour, were now looking tired and turning brown. Rachel slipped off her jacket and hung it on a hook behind the door, dumped her case behind the large pine desk then crossed the room to wash her hands in the small handbasin. Danielle had said she looked pale. Curiously she peered at herself in the mirror above the basin, critically surveying her appearance. Brown eyes stared solemnly back from beneath her fringe of honey-blonde hair. She didn't think she looked particularly pale, although she had most certainly had a shock, seeing Nick again. Would he have found her changed after all this time? There were bound to be differences—after all, it had been a long time since they'd seen each other. She'd slimmed down a little, her features losing the roundness of her teen years, and there were a few tiny lines around her eyes, a result, no doubt of the long hours spent on duty as a hospital doctor.

And what of Nick himself—he'd changed, too, hadn't he? She frowned slightly as she tried to recall. He seemed more powerfully built now in his thirties than he had before and his features more defined somehow, but his colouring was as dark as it had ever been and those eyes—well, there was no changing those. She gave a little shiver as she remembered how he had looked at her, the gaze every bit as challenging and uncompromising as it had ever been. But then there had been that brief moment of wicked laughter and with a thrill she'd all but forgotten she'd been reminded anew of how it had once been between them.

It had never been like that with Jeremy. Carefully she dried her hands then, crossing the room again, she sat down at her desk, switched on her computer and drew the bundle of patient records towards her, reading the name on the top one and smiling as she did so before pressing the buzzer that indicated to the reception staff that she was ready to start her afternoon surgery.

Moments later Tommy Page came into the room, accompanied by his mother Eileen. Tommy had suffered brain damage at birth that had left him with severe learning difficulties and now at twenty-eight he still lived at home with his mother, although on three days a week he attended a local day centre.

'Hello, Tommy.' Rachel smiled. 'Come and sit down and tell me how I can help you today.' This was Tommy's third visit to the surgery in the short time that Rachel had been in Westhampstead.

'Sore throat,' he said. Sitting down in one of the chairs beside Rachel's desk, he unwound the football scarf he was wearing and pointed to his throat.

'How long have you had this sore throat, Tommy?' asked Rachel, glancing at his mother, knowing that Tommy was given to exaggeration.

'He says for the last couple of days,' said Eileen. 'I'm sorry, Dr Beresford, but he insisted on coming to see you.'

'It's all right,' said Rachel reassuringly. 'Now, Tommy, I think I'd better have a look at your throat.' Tommy opened his mouth and allowed Rachel to insert a flat wooden stick, obediently issuing the 'ah' sound she requested.

'Your throat doesn't seem too bad,' she said at last, after gently testing the glands on either side of his neck.

'It really hurts,' Tommy said, obviously fearful now that Rachel didn't believe him.

'I'm sure it does, Tommy,' she said. 'I think you may have a cold developing so what I want you to do is to drink plenty of warm fluids and suck some throat pastilles.' She looked at Eileen. 'If he starts to run a temperature give him soluble paracetamol every four hours.'

'Very well, Doctor.' Eileen stood up. 'I hope we haven't wasted your time.'

'Of course you haven't,' Rachel replied, then, looking at Tommy, she said, 'Have you been to the day centre today, Tommy?'

'No, because of my sore throat,' Tommy replied.

'They've been very good to him,' said Eileen. 'They've even fixed him up with a computer so he can play games at home.'

'Computer,' said Tommy, pointing to Rachel's.

'Yes.' Rachel smiled. 'Just like mine. That's wonderful, Tommy.'

'Come on, Tommy,' said his mother, taking his hand, 'we mustn't take up any more of Dr Beresford's time.'

'Bye, Tommy,' said Rachel.

Just before the door closed behind them she heard Tommy say to his mother, 'She's ever so nice, Dr Rachel.'

'Yes, Tommy, she is,' his mother agreed.

'I love her,' said Tommy.

With a smile Rachel pressed the buzzer for the next patient.

Steadily she worked through the list. There were many

people in Westhampstead who had been patients of Rachel's father and who remembered Rachel as a child, and it seemed to her that these early surgeries of her days at the centre sometimes took far longer than they should as people reminisced or wanted to know where she had been working. Some, she suspected, even came out of curiosity, perhaps for a second opinion, or to see if Rachel was anything like her father had been as a GP.

'So, how is he now—your father?' One such patient came towards the end of that afternoon surgery, a woman called Peggy Reilly who had known Rachel since she'd been a baby and who indeed had been a patient of her father.

'He's very well, thank you, Peggy,' Rachel replied, wondering as she did so whether she should issue a bulletin on her father, which could perhaps be posted in Reception for the benefit of all those who wished to know.

'And what about your poor mother?' Peggy's voice lowered sympathetically.

'Well, Mum's health is not as good as it once was.' Rachel knew there was no point in denying it—her mother's forgetfulness and deteriorating health were well known amongst the residents of the town. 'But Dad looks after her beautifully.'

'I'm sure he does,' Peggy agreed, 'but it can't be easy.'

'Well…' Rachel gave a little shrug. 'Now, how can I help you, Peggy?'

'It's my arthritis playing up again, Doctor. It happens every year about this time—the temperature drops a bit, the evenings begin to draw in and my old joints give me gyp. And I have to say my usual tablets don't seem to be helping at all.'

'Right,' said Rachel, 'let's have a look at your medication chart and see if there are any changes that we can make—there are several new anti-inflammatory drugs on the market so I'm sure we'll be able to find one that suits you.'

At the end of surgery Rachel made her way downstairs to Reception where she found one of the receptionists, Julie Newton, leaning across the desk, talking to a man. As she approached the desk the man turned his head and she saw it was Julie's husband Philip.

'Ah,' said Julie, looking round, 'here's Rachel—I'm sure she'll buy a ticket.'

'What's this?' Rachel smiled at Philip.

'It's a draw for more equipment at the day centre,' Philip explained. 'One of the prizes is a weekend in a luxury hotel—with me.'

'Philip!' Julie exclaimed, and the other receptionists laughed.

'Only joking,' said Philip with a grin. 'But you still get the luxury weekend and there are plenty of other really good prizes.'

'I'll buy some,' said Rachel. Rummaging through her shoulder-bag, she produced a five-pound note and took the pen Julie offered her.

'That's generous of you,' said Philip as she began filling in her details.

'I think the day centre does a fantastic job,' Rachel replied, mindful of Tommy Page and his computer.

'Can I just say I think it's great that you've come back to Westhampstead?' Philip added.

'Thank you, Philip.' Rachel glanced up. 'How's your mum these days?'

'Not so bad.' He paused, his head on one side as if

reminiscing. 'We had some fun in those days, didn't we?' he said at last.

'Eh? What's all this?' Danielle looked from one to the other.

'My mum was housekeeper for Dr and Mrs Beresford,' Philip explained. 'We lived up at Ashton House when I was a kid.'

'Oh,' said Danielle, 'I didn't know that.'

'Shall I fill in the rest of those for you, Rachel?' asked Julie as Rachel began to fill in the second counterfoil.

'Thanks, Julie,' Rachel replied, pushing the counterfoils and the pen across the desk and stuffing the tickets into her bag. 'I am in a bit of a rush—as usual.' She pulled a face. 'I must go. Nice to see you again, Philip. Say hello to your mum for me.' With that she hurried out of the centre and into her car to make the two house calls she needed to do before she could go home.

Home for Rachel, as she had told Nick Kowalski, was a house in Cathedral Close, which she was renting for a year from friends of her parents who were travelling abroad. Tucked away in one corner of the close in the lee of the great cathedral, St Edmund's was an elegant, stone-built Georgian-style house filled with antiques, and if the furnishings were a little too traditional for Rachel's more modern tastes it was something she felt she could live with. Some of the more expensive pieces of glass and porcelain she had locked away in the glass-fronted cabinets in the dining room, terrified that she might break them, but after a while she had begun to relax and enjoy the undeniable comfort and luxury of the house. In many ways it was similar to Ashton House, her parents' home, but it had been many years since she had lived there and she had since become used to a more modest way of life, first in student then hospital accommodation and more recently in the apartment she had shared with Jeremy.

As she thought of Jeremy she kicked off her shoes and sank down onto one of the two deep, comfortable sofas. When she had first met Jeremy, a fellow doctor in the practice where she had been working, and had brought him home to meet her parents, he had been hailed as a perfect match for her and the perfect son-in-law for them. The son of wealthy parents, educated at one of the country's top public schools and with a career that looked set to take him to his own Harley Street practice, he must have seemed like the answer to Rachel's parents' prayers, but for Rachel things hadn't quite worked out that way. She was fond of Jeremy, of course she was, but somehow their relationship had become static, with neither of them seemingly interested in marriage or starting a family, which, from Rachel's point of view at least, was strange because she knew deep in her heart that she wanted both of those—to be married and to have children. But somehow she'd never been able to visualise either with Jeremy. They were friends, good friends, but that was all and their relationship seemed to lack the extra spark that Rachel felt sure should be there if any further commitment was to be made.

The spark had been there with Nick. The thought, unbidden, came into her mind. Why should she think of that now? Only because she had seen him again that day, she told herself fiercely. Her relationship—if you could even call it that—with Nick had been years ago. They had both been very young and they had both, without a doubt, changed in the intervening years. But that spark had been there. It had been there all those years ago, it had been there every time he had as much as looked at her and even more so whenever he had touched her. And her skin, without fail, had tingled in response, and it had been there again today.

She gave an angry little gesture as the realisation hit her. It was ridiculous that she should even think such a thing. It had simply been the shock of seeing him again after all that time that had done it—nothing more at all. Nick Kowalski was bad news. He'd been bad news then with his high-speed motorbike and his wild ways and he was probably bad news now. It was surprising that he'd done so well in the police force—he was young to be a DCI but, no doubt, he had ridden roughshod over anyone who had got in his way on his passage through the ranks. Somehow she couldn't quite think of him as an utterly reformed character. No doubt his wife had suffered—by his own admission his marriage had ended in divorce— and there was a child, a little girl. She couldn't imagine Nick as a father but his face had softened when he'd mentioned his daughter.

But what in the world was she thinking about Nick for anyway? Hadn't he hurt her before—dumped her unceremoniously without so much as a word of explanation, leaving her desolate? The last thing she wanted now was to have too many dealings with him. That she might have to spend time with him occasionally in her work with the police was quite enough, although with a bit of luck even that shouldn't be too often. Rachel knew from experience that most of her work would be not with plainclothes CID officers but with the uniformed station staff and, provided that Westhampstead was still the quiet country town it had always been, she saw little reason that should change.

With that slightly reassuring thought uppermost in her mind, she stood up and made her way into the kitchen where she began preparing pasta and salad for her supper.

She had barely finished eating when her phone rang and, desperately trying to swallow the last mouthful, she answered it, expecting it to be her father or perhaps Jeremy, although she and Jeremy had agreed to have as little contact as possible during this trial separation period.

'Hello?' she said. There was a silence on the other end then the caller hung up. With a little grimace Rachel replaced the receiver, only for the phone to ring again immediately.

'Hello?' she said, 'Who is this?'

'Rachel?'

Her heart jumped. 'Yes…?'

'It's Nick. Nick Kowalski.'

'Oh,' she said, 'hello.' She'd known it was him as soon as he'd spoken her name—had recognised his voice.

'You're eating,' he said abruptly. 'Sorry.'

'No, it's all right,' she said breathlessly. 'I've just finished.'

'I understand you are duty doctor for the station tonight.'

'Yes,' she said. 'That's right.'

'I need a doctor to examine a man who has been brought in for questioning.'

'What's the problem?' She hoped she sounded professional and efficient even though for some extraordinary reason her pulse was racing.

'He seems disorientated and his movements are uncoordinated.'

'Has he been drinking?'

'Not as far as we know.'

'I'll come down now.'

'Thanks.'

'Oh, Nick?' There was a slight pause.

'Yes?'

'Did you phone just now—a moment ago?'

'No. Why?'

'Oh, it doesn't matter—it must have been a wrong number. I'll be with you shortly.'

She hung up and stared at the phone for a moment. Why in the world had she reacted in such a silly way to the sound of Nick's voice? Had it been because she hadn't imagined that he would phone her? But that was stupid—given the fact that she was area police doctor, it was quite on the cards that he might phone her. Usually she would expect it to be the duty sergeant who would do so but it certainly wasn't outside the realms of possibility for a DCI. Hastily she took her dishes to the kitchen then ran upstairs, changed her skirt for a pair of trousers and pulled on a warm sweater before picking up her case and leaving the house. In spite of her earlier conclusions that Nick was bad news and should be avoided at all costs, she found that as she drove to police headquarters her pulse was still racing and she felt a level of excitement at the thought of working with him that she hadn't felt for a very long time.

CHAPTER TWO

IT WAS quite dark by the time she reached police head-quarters, another indication that autumn was almost upon them. Locking her car, Rachel climbed the steps at the front of the building and on opening the main doors found Nick waiting for her in Reception. He looked tense, wound up like a tightly coiled spring, and for one moment she was tempted to apologise in case she'd kept him waiting. Then she thought better of it. This man was not her boss or her superior, she was not answerable to him and it would be as well for her to remember that fact in all her dealings with him.

'Rachel.' He turned on his heel.

'You have a patient for me?' She nodded at the sergeant on the desk, not Harry Mason this time but a younger man who likewise acknowledged her with a nod. 'Yes,' Nick replied curtly, 'come this way.' She followed him out of the reception area down two corridors to the cells at the rear of the building. The place smelt of pine disinfectant. A radio somewhere played rap music and occasional shouts and mutterings could be heard from the cells they passed.

'Has this man been charged?' asked Rachel.

'No, not yet,' Nick replied, 'but I'm anxious to tie this case up—these arrests have come at the end of a lengthy operation involving a large number of my men.'

'So...' Rachel raised one eyebrow. 'Inconvenient that one is sick at the eleventh hour, is that what you're saying?'

'If you want to put it that way.' Nick's jaw tightened.

'Why is he in a cell?'

'Because it seemed the best place—he collapsed and we put him on the nearest bed.'

'Can you tell me anything about his behaviour before the collapse?' she asked.

'Very erratic,' he replied, 'bizarre almost—he was acting as if he was drunk but there was no smell of alcohol. He also seemed to have some sort of tremor which is what led me to suspect this may be a medical problem.' As he finished speaking Nick opened the door to a cell where Rachel could see a man lying on the bed and a uniformed officer standing beside him.

'Do we know his name?' asked Rachel.

'Masters,' Nick replied.

'And his first name?' Rachel bent over the inert form of the man.

'Paul.'

'Paul, can you hear me?' The man's eyes were closed and as Rachel took his wrist she found him to have a rapid pulse. He appeared pale and his skin was cold and clammy to the touch. There was also a distinctive, sweetish smell about him.

'Did he have anything on him to indicate that he may be diabetic?' asked Rachel, checking around his neck to see if he was wearing any sort of tag and failing to find one.

Nick glanced up at the officer who shook his head. 'No, nothing,' he replied, then after a moment's pause, he said, 'Do you think that's what this is?'

'Yes, I do.' Rachel nodded and opened her case. 'A pinprick test will decide it.' Carefully, watched by Nick and the attending officer, she carried out the test then nodded. 'As I thought,' she said, 'his blood sugar's very low—he's in a hypoglycaemic coma.'

'Can you treat that?' asked Nick.

'I can give him an injection.' Rachel opened her case and took out packets containing a syringe and ampoules of dextrose.

Moments later she identified a vein in the man's arm and administered the injection. Almost immediately he began to stir then he opened his eyes.

'Paul,' she said gently after a few moments, 'are you with us again?'

Paul Masters gazed up at her, his expression almost one of disbelief, then as he moved his head and caught sight of Nick and the officer behind him he rolled his eyes and groaned. 'You know something?' he said. 'I thought I'd died and gone to heaven and this was an angel.' He inclined his head in Rachel's direction. 'Then I see your ugly mugs and I know it was all a dream.'

'No, Paul,' said Rachel briskly, 'it wasn't a dream—it was a diabetic coma. Your blood sugar had dropped to a critical low. Don't you wear a tag to alert anyone to the fact that you're diabetic?'

'Yeah, I do,' the man replied rubbing his eyes with one hand, 'but the chain broke—needs fixing.'

'Well, I suggest you get it fixed.' Rachel began clearing up her equipment and medication packaging. 'And that you wear it at all times,' she added. 'So what caused your blood sugar to drop so low—have you missed a meal?'

'Yeah, a couple probably—thanks to this lot.' Paul Masters's gaze flickered to the two police officers.

'If you'd told us you were diabetic we could have taken the appropriate measures,' Nick replied tersely.

'Yeah, right,' Paul Masters grunted. Looking hopefully up at Rachel, he said, 'Are you going to send me to hospital?'

'I don't think that will be necessary,' said Rachel.

'But I need time to recover,' the man began to protest.

'I'm sure DCI Kowalski will give you an hour or so recovery period,' Rachel replied, 'but first I want to check your blood sugar again.'

Ten minutes later Nick escorted Rachel out of the cell, leaving Paul Masters with the officer. 'Was that really necessary?' he asked as they reached Reception.

'What?' Rachel frowned, thinking he was questioning her treatment or diagnosis of the patient.

'The period of recovery.'

'Probably not.' She gave a little shrug. 'But it's better to be on the safe side in these matters. I also suggest he is given something to eat.'

'Would a three-course meal be sufficient?' There was a trace of sarcasm in Nick's voice now.

'A couple of rounds of cheese sandwiches should do the trick,' Rachel replied sweetly.

'As if he hasn't wasted enough police time as it is,' muttered Nick.

'You think he put himself into a coma deliberately?' Rachel raised her eyebrows.

'I wouldn't put it past him. Let's face it, he wasn't wearing his tag and he must know he shouldn't miss meals...'

'Even so—it's a bit drastic.' She paused. 'Anyway, an hour is not that long.'

'In that case, you won't mind coming and having a drink with me,' Nick retorted swiftly.

'I'm sorry?' She stared at him.

'You've put me in this position of having an hour to

kill—I would say the least you could do is to keep me company in the meantime.'

'Oh, I don't think…' she began, desperately trying to think of an excuse, any excuse, not to go with him. 'I have things to do.' It was the last thing she wanted, to establish any sort of relationship with him other than a purely professional one.

Nick, it seemed, had other ideas. 'Nonsense,' he said firmly, then after a brief word to the duty sergeant he took her elbow and propelled her out of the station doors. 'What could be more important than renewing acquaintance with an old friend?'

Weakly Rachel allowed herself to be guided down the steps of the police station and a hundred or so yards down the street towards a sign, which swayed and creaked in the wind and stated quite clearly that the Red Lion served the finest ale in town. It was warm inside with a welcome from a crackling log fire, and briefly the chatter from the locals gathered around the bar ceased as they recognised Nick and curiously eyed Rachel up and down.

'What'll you have?' Nick half turned to her.

'A lager would be nice,' she replied.

'There's a table over there in the corner.' Nick nodded towards an alcove on the far side of the room. 'I'll bring the drinks over.'

Almost with a sense of unreality Rachel sat down and looked around the pub with its low beamed ceiling and flagstoned floor. If anyone had told her only the day before that she would be sitting here sharing a drink with Nick Kowalski, she would never have believed it. She watched him as he turned from the bar carrying two glasses and crossed the floor, placed the drinks on the table and sat down opposite her. Taking a deep breath, he lifted his glass.

'Cheers.'

'Yes,' Rachel replied, 'cheers.' Lifting her own glass, she took a sip as Nick did likewise.

They were silent for a moment as if each of them was searching for something to say. As their eyes met across the table it was Nick who broke the silence. 'It really is good to see you again, Rachel, after all this time.'

'Yes, Nick.' She nodded. 'It's good to see you as well.' Suddenly she realised she meant it—it *was* good to see him in spite of what had happened.

'We had some good times, didn't we?' he said softly.

'Yes,' she agreed, 'we did.' There was something in his eyes now that was decidedly disconcerting and wildly she grabbed her glass again and took another mouthful—too much this time, which caused her to cough. 'But…' she spluttered, 'it…it was all a very long time ago.'

'True.' Nick nodded. 'Even so, there are some things you never forget.' He paused, took another mouthful of his own drink then set his glass down again and leaned back in his chair. 'Tell me,' he said, 'about this relationship you are in now…the one you feel isn't going anywhere.'

Rachel shrugged. 'What do you want to know?'

'Well, for a start, who is the lucky man?'

'His name is Jeremy Lisle,' she replied reluctantly, 'he's a doctor.'

'Ah, very appropriate.'

'What do you mean?' She stared at him.

'For you,' he said, 'and for your parents, of course. I'm sure they approve.'

'Well, yes, they like Jeremy…'

'Now, why doesn't that come as a surprise?' Nick lifted his head and laughed. It was the same easygoing, infectious laugh she remembered so well and which for a long time had haunted her dreams. 'I'm sure they see a doctor as far more suitable marriage material for their only daughter than a mere garage hand with a rather dodgy reputation to boot.' He paused. 'Although, from what you say, it doesn't sound as if there are wedding bells in the air.' When she didn't reply he lowered his head, tilting it to one side in order to look into her face. 'Rachel…?'

She took a deep breath. She didn't really want to discuss Jeremy or her relationship with anyone, least of all Nick. 'No,' she said coolly, 'I don't think there will be any wedding bells, at least not in the foreseeable future.'

'You said this morning that you felt the relationship wasn't going anywhere.'

'Did I?' How she wished she hadn't said that. She'd hoped he might have forgotten it but it seemed there was no chance of that. She shrugged. 'Well, let's say it had all become a bit static and when the chance of this job came up—'

'You grabbed it?' He raised innocent eyebrows.

'Well, no, not quite like that, but I thought it might be an opportunity to get a better perspective on things…' She trailed off as she saw his lips twitch.

'You make it sound like a business arrangement,' he said.

'It's not,' she replied hotly, 'of course it's not!'

'No, I'm sure it isn't.' He paused again reflectively then said, 'And this guy, what did you say his name was—Julian?'

'Jeremy.'

'Oh, yes, Jeremy, that's right. Well, what does he think of this perspective exercise?'

'As it happens, he's in full agreement with it,' she replied.

'Wouldn't suit me.' Nick folded his arms and shook his head.

'No, Nick, I'm sure it wouldn't.' She paused then mercilessly she said, 'So tell me about your wife.'

'My wife?' He looked up sharply. 'I don't have a wife.'

'I know. You're divorced now, you said, but you were married once. I understand she was the daughter of a friend of your mother.'

'How in the world did you know that?' He stared at her.

'I heard it somewhere,' she said vaguely, not wanting to tell him that it had been her own mother who had told her, relating the news to her with a decided note of relief and satisfaction in her voice. 'Did I know her?'

'I doubt it,' he said. 'Her name is Marilyn—she was Marilyn Rooney.'

'I remember the Rooney family,' said Rachel slowly.

'Yes, well, Marilyn and I went to the same school— Westhampstead High—a bit different from your posh boarding school for young ladies.'

'Still taking the mickey?' she said coolly. 'You always did if I remember rightly.'

'Not at all,' he replied firmly. 'It was quite something for me—a no-hoper from the wrong side of town to be going out with the local doctor's daughter. My poor old mum never did quite get over it. She used to worry about the wedding—you didn't know that, did you?' He looked at Rachel and chuckled. 'But she did—not that she need have worried in the end, the way things turned out. Marilyn's and my wedding was a very low-key affair…registry office, then down the local for a bit of a knees-up.'

'How *is* your mum, Nick?' Desperately Rachel interrupted him, not wanting to hear these details of his marriage.

He stopped in mid-sentence and stared at her while behind them someone began feeding coins into a fruit machine. 'My mum died four years ago,' he said at last.

'Oh, Nick.' Her hand flew to her mouth and she stared at him, instantly recalling the bustling little woman who had shown her nothing but kindness on many occasions. 'I'm so sorry, I didn't know.'

'No,' he said, and there was a touch of bitterness in his tone now. 'I don't suppose your parents thought to let you know that.'

'I liked your mum,' she said slowly. 'I really did.'

'She liked you as well,' he said simply. 'In spite of the fact that she was in total awe of your situation and background, she really liked you. She thought you were a lovely girl.'

'Did she like Marilyn?' Rachel leaned forward slightly and noticed that at mention of his ex-wife's name Nick's jaw tightened and a bleak expression came into his eyes.

'I don't know really.' He gave a slight shrug. 'I suppose she did. Maud Rooney was her friend so, yes, I dare say she liked her daughter—we never really discussed it.'

'So what happened between you and Marilyn?' she asked tentatively at last. From wanting to know nothing, for some reason she now suddenly needed to know more.

His expression changed yet again, his eyebrows drawing together in a black line, and just for a moment Rachel wished she hadn't asked.

'We weren't suited,' he muttered. 'Incompatible is the word used, I believe. Marilyn wanted a stay-at-home guy with a nine-to-five job. Someone who would always be there in the evenings and at weekends—that sort of thing.'

'And that wasn't you?'

'Not once I'd joined the police force it wasn't—if it ever was. I don't know.' He shrugged and just for a moment Rachel witnessed something in his eyes that summed up the bleakness of his marriage.

'So what made you join the police force?' she asked in an attempt to draw the conversation away from Marilyn.

He didn't speak immediately, instead toying with his glass as if deliberating on whether to answer her question or not. Then, his jaw tightening again, he said, 'Actually, believe it or not, Rachel, it was a remark your mother made to your father that I happened to overhear that was the cause.'

'Really?' Rachel stared at him in astonishment.

'Yes.' He nodded. 'It was one evening when I called for you and I was waiting in the hallway of Ashton House. I don't know whether they knew I was there or not—the housekeeper, Mrs Newton, had let me in. Anyway, I heard your mother say that I was a no-hoper who would never amount to anything—''a waster'' was the expression she used, I think.'

Rachel stared at him. 'Oh Nick,' she said at last, 'I'm sorry.'

'No,' he said quickly, 'don't be sorry. It was the kick up the pants I needed. From that moment my mission in life was to prove her wrong.'

'And you've done just that,' she said softly. 'Look at you—there can't be too many DCIs of your age.'

He shrugged. 'I don't know about that.'

'It was a shame your marriage had to suffer as a consequence though.'

'I don't know.' He shook his head. 'Sometimes I wonder if it would have worked even if I wasn't in the force—Marilyn and I were like chalk and cheese really.'

'But you have a daughter?' she said gently.

'Oh, yes.' His expression softened at mention of his daughter. 'I have Lucy. She was the reason Marilyn and I married in the first place. She's the light of my life. You'll meet her.'

'I hope I shall but, Nick, I really do need to go now.' She glanced at her watch as she spoke then drained her glass and stood up.

'Yes,' he said, doing likewise. 'I suppose I'd better get back as well and see if our friend is ready to cooperate.' He stood aside to allow Rachel to pass him but as she did so he caught her hand. Startled, she looked at him, unable to read the expression that had come into his eyes. 'It really is good to see you again, Rachel,' he said softly.

'And you, Nick.' Her voice was suddenly husky and as he applied a quick pressure to her hand, her skin tingled—just as it had always done at his touch.

It had shaken Rachel, seeing Nick again after all these years, and in spite of the fact that she had made up her mind from the outset that theirs was to be a purely professional relationship, she knew it might not be as easy as she had at first thought.

To her dismay she found herself looking for him in the town, when she was shopping or out on house calls, and when she was on call she found herself willing the phone to ring to say that her services were required at police headquarters. When one such call did come, it was late on a Saturday night and she was called to attend a victim of a street brawl who had collapsed. To her shame, on receiving the call, her adrenalin level soared at the thought of seeing Nick again and she reached police headquarters in record time, only to find that Nick wasn't involved, probably wasn't even there, and that the uniformed staff were in charge.

After that she tried to get a grip on herself and put him out of her mind. After all, what they had once been to each other had been a very long time ago and no doubt in the intervening years they had both become different people. It didn't stop her remembering, though, and sometimes as she drove around town memories of that distant time came back in disturbing waves: the rides on Nick's motorbike late at night; the old cinema— a snooker hall now—where they had always sat in the back row; the café in the high street—a building society had its offices there now—where they had congregated with other bikers to play rock music on the jukebox and drink endless cups of coffee. And then, of course, there was the park where they'd walked late at night, arms around each other, and where invariably they ended up on the mossy ground beneath the trees and had loved each other passionately under the stars.

As each new memory was rekindled a fresh surge of emotion was released, leaving Rachel in a strange, highly strung state not at all like her usual calm and collected self.

One evening just as she had finished surgery Danielle buzzed through to say there was a call for her.

'Put them through,' she replied automatically, and before she even had time to wonder who it might be she heard a voice at the other end, a voice she instantly recognised. 'Georgie?' she cried in delight.

'Rachel! Oh this is wonderful. I heard today that you were back in town. I didn't believe it at first, I said, no, that couldn't be right, that you were up in Southport or Stockport or somewhere—but they said you were right here in Westhampstead.'

'But what are you doing here?' Rachel demanded, 'the last time I heard about *you*, you were backpacking in Peru, or on a banana boat up the Limpopo or somewhere equally obscure.'

'Oh, I was. I was,' cried Georgie, 'but I'm home for a while. Poor old pops is not too well and I'm keeping an eye on him. But what about you—where are you living? Are you at Ashton House?'

'Lord, no,' Rachel replied. 'I'm renting an enchanting little house in Cathedral Close. Listen, why don't you come over?'

'When?'

'What about tonight? I could cook us something and we could have a girly night in—just like we used to.'

'Sounds wonderful—I'll bring some wine.'

Five minutes later Rachel had finished signing her repeat prescriptions and had almost cleared her in-tray. She and Georgina Reynolds had started school on the same day and had been friends ever since. There was very little they didn't know about each other and as far as Rachel was concerned the idea of an evening of catching up and girly gossip with Georgie was the best thing that could happen in her present rather fragile state of mind.

She took the last envelope from the in-tray and saw that it had been hand-delivered and was addressed to Dr

Rachel Beresford and marked 'Personal', which presumably was why it hadn't been opened and dealt with by the staff. Quickly she slit open the envelope, imagining it to be a request for medication or something similar, but when she drew out the single piece of paper and unfolded it she found it was neither. Written in pencil in childish print it simply said: *I love you Rachel.*

She stared at it, unable for a moment to believe quite what she was seeing, and then she remembered Tommy Page and what he had said to his mother when he had left the surgery a few days previously. In that moment she guessed that it must have been Tommy who had written this note. With a little smile she folded the sheet of paper and slipped it into the drawer of her desk then, with a last look around her consulting room, she switched off the light and went out.

'Actually, Rachel, there's something I think you should know.' Georgina peered at her from beneath her cloud of frizzy dark hair.

'Oh?' Rachel set her wine glass down on the coffee table and raised one eyebrow, suspecting that she knew exactly what her friend was about to tell her.

'I don't know quite how to tell you really…' Georgie went on.

'Is it about Nick Kowalski and the fact that he's back in town?' Rachel leaned back and rested her head against the sofa cushions.

'Well, yes.' Georgie stared at her in surprise. 'But how did you know that was what I was going to say?'

'Probably because you are the only person who knew exactly how I felt about him—that's why,' Rachel replied calmly. 'And likewise,' she went on, 'you are the only one who would know how his presence in Westhampstead would affect me.'

'And has it?' asked Georgie curiously. 'Affected you, I mean?'

'Is there any point denying it?' Rachel pulled a face.

'Not with me there isn't.' Georgie grinned but it was a sympathetic grin. 'But surely you won't need to see him,' she went on after a moment. 'I know Westhampstead isn't that big, but—'

'I've taken over Steve O'Malley's police duties,' Rachel said flatly.

'And Nick Kowalski is…? Oh, no, you're not going to tell me he's stationed at the headquarters here.'

'You've got it in one.' Rachel nodded ruefully.

'Oh, Rach.' Georgie stared at her again then, leaning forward, she picked up the bottle of wine and topped up both glasses. 'So, have you seen him yet?'

'Oh, yes.' Rachel nodded. 'A couple of times, actually.'

'And…?'

'And what?' Rachel stared into her glass.

'Well, how did you feel?' Georgie demanded.

'How do you think I felt?'

'Don't know really.' Georgie shrugged. 'I know you were besotted with the guy once but, let's face it, Rach, that *was* a long time ago and, well…I guess everyone's moved on a bit since then.'

'Yes, I suppose.' Rachel sighed and briefly closed her eyes.

Georgie frowned. 'Well, for a start, he's married, isn't he?'

'Divorced.' She opened her eyes again.

'Oh, really? I didn't know that. I guess I'm out of touch as well.' Georgie paused, sipping her wine thoughtfully. Then, drawing up her legs and tucking them beneath her on the sofa, she said, 'But you have Jeremy now.'

'Do I?' Rachel stared into her glass again.

'Well, don't you?' Georgie demanded, when Rachel failed to add anything.

'I don't know really.' She looked up at last and shrugged. 'Jeremy and I have been going through a rough patch recently,' she said. 'We both agreed that this time apart might help us to sort ourselves out.'

'Oh, Rachel, I'm so sorry, I had no idea.' Georgie reached out and touched her arm, and to her dismay Rachel felt the tears prickle at the back of her eyes.

'It wasn't going anywhere, Georgie,' she said after a moment. 'Jeremy doesn't want to settle down and have a family.'

'And you do?'

'Yes, I do. And I don't want to leave it until it's too late—I've seen too much of that in my surgery. Women of our age group who pour everything into their careers and put marriage and children on hold, then when finally they get around to it their bodies rebel and say no way.'

'Maybe this will bring Jeremy to his senses,' said Georgie.

'Yes, maybe.' Rachel shrugged again. 'Trouble is, I'm not even sure about that any more. Jeremy, I mean...'

They were silent for a while then Rachel looked up again. 'How about you?' she said.

'How about me?' Georgie wrinkled her nose.

'Well, is there anyone in your life at the moment? Wasn't it Scott someone?'

'Scott was a ski instructor,' Georgie replied, 'and that was months ago. It's Robbie now,' she added with a wicked little grin.

'Robbie?'

'Yes, I met him in Peru and he's gorgeous.'

'You say that about them all.' Rachel smiled weakly.

'I know I do.' Georgie sighed, growing serious again. 'But maybe, just maybe, this will be the one…'

They were silent again, each reflecting on their past and the men they had loved, then suddenly Rachel spoke again, changing the subject. 'Did you say your father wasn't too well?'

'Yes.' Georgie nodded. 'I'm not sure what's wrong— he went for some tests a couple of months ago and there didn't seem to be anything too wrong then, but he really isn't right now.'

'He's on Steve's list, isn't he?' said Rachel.

'Yes, he is.'

'Would you like me to call round and see him?'

'Oh, Rachel, yes. Yes, please, I was hoping you would say that.' Georgie looked relieved. 'It's so hard to get him to go to the centre but if you were to just call in for a chat and a cup of tea I'm sure he would be delighted—he's very fond of you.'

'And I of him,' Rachel smiled. 'So that's settled, then.'

'If only everything were as simple.' Georgie sighed. 'Tell me, what are you going to do about Nick?'

'What can I do?' Rachel shrugged. 'I've resigned myself that I'll have to see him and work with him from time to time.'

'What will you do if he wants to take it further?'

'What do you mean, take it further?' Rachel frowned.

'Well, if he asks you out—for a drink or something, you know, for old times' sake, that sort of thing.'

'Actually,' she said, 'as it happens…'

'You're not going to tell me that's already happened!'

Georgie sat up straight, clutching a cushion which she hugged against her body.

'Yes.' Rachel nodded, a little shamefaced.

'Wow! Well, I must say, the pair of you didn't waste any time getting it together again.'

'It wasn't like that!' protested Rachel.

'So what was it like?' Georgie demanded. 'Go on, tell me.'

'I was called out to see a patient in police custody. Nick was in charge of the case…'

'Was that the first time you'd seen him since you came back?'

'No,' Rachel explained, 'I'd seen him earlier when I went to police headquarters to familiarise myself with the place.'

'So it wasn't as much of a shock as it might have been.' Georgie paused and peered at Rachel. 'But was it a shock that first time?'

'Yes,' Rachel admitted ruefully, 'it was. A real shock. I had no idea he was back in Westhampstead.'

'So, go on. What happened this next time?' Georgie was agog now.

'He asked me to go for a drink with him after I'd seen the patient—that's all. We went to the Red Lion…and, well, we sort of caught up on what each of us has been doing for the last however many years it is since we last saw each other.'

'You were mad about him, Rach,'

'Yes,' Rachel agreed, 'I know I was.'

'And he was about you as well…'

'So much so that he married someone else,' said Rachel bitterly.

'Not immediately he didn't,' Georgie protested.

'Maybe not.' Rachel shrugged.

'So what did happen between you?' asked Georgie curiously. 'What ended it? I never really knew. You just told me it was over and that you didn't want to talk about it.'

'He just stopped writing to me—that's all.'

'No explanation or anything?'

'No, nothing.'

'Didn't you ask him why?' asked Georgie almost in disbelief.

'I was going to,' she said, 'and then I heard, well, I heard he was going out with someone else so in the end I didn't do anything.'

'This someone else, was it Marilyn Rooney—the one he married?'

'I don't know.' Rachel shook her head. 'I don't think so…I'm not sure.'

'How did you feel at the time?'

'I was heartbroken,' Rachel admitted. 'Devastated really. I didn't come back to Westhampstead for a long time after that.'

'So how *did* you feel this time, when you saw him again?'

'All right, I suppose.' Rachel wrinkled her nose.

'Rach, this is me you're talking to,' said Georgie. 'Now, tell me how you really felt.'

'Honestly?'

'Yes, honestly.'

'Cross my heart and hope to die honestly?'

'Yes, cross your heart and hope to die honestly.'

'I…I…well, I suppose really, if I'm really honest…it's knocked me for six,' she admitted at last, 'and truthfully, Georgie, I don't really know what I'm going to do about it.'

CHAPTER THREE

'JULIE, there was a plain envelope in my tray last night marked "Personal"—have you any idea who handed it in?' Rachel had been about to leave on her house calls but she paused at the reception desk.

'No. Sorry.' Julie shook her head then turned to Danielle, who was checking and filing patient records. 'Do you know, Danielle?'

'It was in the outside mail box,' Danielle replied, 'where people leave their repeat prescription requests when we are closed. I particularly noticed it because it was marked personal—that's why I didn't open it,' she added. Her voice had taken on an anxious note and Rachel hastened to reassure her.

'That's quite all right,' she said, 'I just wondered if any of you saw who handed it in, that's all.'

'Didn't it say who it was from?' asked Julie with a frown.

'No.' Rachel shook her head. 'It didn't.'

'It wasn't a repeat prescription form, then?' asked Danielle.

'No, it was simply a handwritten note—without a signature.'

'I wish people wouldn't do that,' grumbled Julie. 'They put grubby little scraps of paper in the box asking for more of "that ointment you gave me for my piles", and not only are we expected to know which ointment they are talking about, we are also expected to know

who it's for. Is that the sort of thing you got, Rachel?'
she added.

'Something like that, yes.' Rachel nodded vaguely.
For some reason she didn't want the staff to know that
it wasn't a request for medication she'd received.
Neither did she want to have to say that she suspected
the note was from Tommy Page. Instead, she turned her
attention to the patient records that Danielle passed
across the desk.

'That's today's house calls,' the receptionist said. 'I
should take an umbrella with you if I were you. It's
absolutely chucking it down out there.'

'Right.' Rachel peered out of the main entrance and
saw that it was indeed raining hard. Picking up her case
and opening the main doors, she made a quick dash for
her car. Her calls that morning included a new mother
and baby who had just been discharged from hospital,
an elderly man in the final stages of terminal cancer and
a woman suffering from emphysema. All were, of
course, patients of Steve O'Malley and only the wife of
the elderly man knew who Rachel was and asked after
her father. When she had seen the final patient she returned to her car and picked up a further set of records,
which she had taken from the files earlier and studied.
These belonged to Georgie's father, Harvey Reynolds,
whom Rachel had promised to visit.

The Reynolds family home was tucked away at the
end of a long drive—a Tudor-style house set in beautifully tended gardens, which perfectly befitted Harvey's
status as a retired university don. Georgie's mother had
died when Georgie had been in her teens and her father
had never remarried, choosing instead to live alone.

After Rachel had parked the car at the front entrance

and rung the bell, Georgie herself opened the door. 'Rachel!' she cried. 'You came.'

'I said I would, didn't I?' Rachel smiled.

'Yes, I know, but…' Georgie threw an anxious glance over her shoulder. 'I don't want him to think I've asked you to come specifically.'

'I don't know what you're talking about,' said Rachel briskly. 'I've come for coffee and a chat—surely an old friend can do that?'

'Bless you,' murmured Georgie.

'Who is it, Georgie?' Harvey appeared in the hallway behind her, a still handsome man even now in his seventies, with thick white hair and striking blue eyes. 'Why,' he exclaimed, his face lighting up, 'it's Rachel. Georgie said you were back. How lovely to see you again, my dear.'

Together they made their way into a pleasant drawing room that overlooked the garden then Georgie took herself off to the kitchen to make the coffee. They chatted briefly of Rachel's return to Westhampstead, of her own parents and of her mother's fragile health, and then carefully, subtly Rachel tried to draw the conversation round to Harvey himself. 'The garden is still looking good, Harvey,' she said, standing up and walking to the window.

'It's rather bedraggled today with all this rain. Mind you, it's not before time—we needed it.'

'Just as long as it knows when to stop,' Rachel replied with a laugh then casually added, 'Do you still do the gardening yourself, Harvey?'

'Not as much as I used to,' he admitted. 'I have a man come in these days to give me a hand with the heavy stuff. I'm not as young as I used to be, Rachel.'

'My father says exactly the same thing,' said Rachel

with a nod. 'The trouble with him is he doesn't know when to ease up.'

'And that's why you're here, isn't it, my dear?' Harvey's blue eyes twinkled. 'To tell me I'm getting past it and that I should be thinking of easing up a bit.' As Rachel opened her mouth to protest, he lifted one hand to stop her. 'I'm not stupid, you know,' he went on, 'I know it was that girl of mine who asked you to call in to see me.'

'Do you know something, Harvey?' said Rachel with a laugh. 'You have just made things a whole lot easier for me. We can stop pretending now and you can tell me how you really are.'

By the time Georgie returned with the coffee Rachel had established that Harvey was experiencing symptoms that could indicate a heart problem and had arranged for him to attend her surgery for a thorough examination and blood tests.

'Thanks, Rach,' Georgie whispered when half an hour later Rachel walked to the front door with her friend. 'There was no way he was going to come to the centre off his own bat. But...' Her eyes clouded anxiously. 'You don't think it's anything too serious...?'

'Let's not speculate until we know for certain,' Rachel replied. 'The tests should tell us more.' As she finished speaking her mobile phone suddenly went off and she took it out of her pocket. 'Excuse me,' she said to Georgie. 'I need to answer this.'

'Of course,' Georgie murmured, and moved discreetly away.

'Rachel?' It was Nick. There was no disguising his voice, neither was there any denying the way her heart lurched.

'Yes.' She swallowed.

'You are duty for us today, aren't you?'

'Yes,' she replied, 'I am.'

'Good. We need you to certify a death.'

'Give me the address,' she said, aware now that Georgie had turned and was watching her.

'There isn't an address as such,' he replied. 'A body has just been recovered from undergrowth.'

'Oh, I see. Where do I come to?'

'The towpath beyond Millar's Wharf—I'll meet you. How soon can you be there?'

Rachel glanced at her watch. 'Fifteen minutes?' she said.

'OK. See you then.' He hung up.

'That was him, wasn't it?' Georgie demanded as Rachel ended the call and turned to her. 'Nick. Nick Kowalski.'

'I… How…?'

'No need to ask me how I knew,' said Georgie with a grin. 'It's written all over your face. You never were very good at hiding anything like that—especially from me.'

It was still raining when Rachel arrived at Millar's Wharf and parked her car on a large patch of wasteland alongside several police vehicles. As she switched off her engine and stepped from the car Nick climbed out of an unmarked vehicle and crossed to meet her. He was dressed in dark clothes, the collar of his black bomber jacket turned up against the relentless rain.

'Don't you have a coat?' His tone was faintly incredulous as his gaze travelled over her, taking in the suit she invariably wore for work and her neat shoes—totally unsuitable for scrabbling about in undergrowth on wet towpaths.

'I was on house calls,' she replied coolly, thankful that

she had remembered the advice of the senior partner in her previous practice who had told her always to be prepared for any eventuality when working with the police. 'But, yes, I do have other clothing with me.' Moving to the rear of her car, she unlocked the boot and under Nick's watchful gaze drew out a green waxed jacket with a hood and a pair of sturdy rubber boots. She pulled on the jacket and set the boots on the ground. Stepping out of one of her shoes, she would have overbalanced in a sudden gust of wind if Nick hadn't stepped forward and steadied her by taking her arm.

'Thanks.' She pulled a face, feeling suddenly foolish and expecting Nick to laugh at her ungainly action, but his face remained deadly serious and Rachel was reminded of exactly why they were there.

'Do we know any details?' she asked as she closed the boot, pulled up her hood and picked up her case.

'The body is that of a young woman,' Nick replied as they fell into step and began crossing the waste ground in the direction of the towpath and the canal. 'We think it is probably that of the girl who was reported missing a few days ago.'

'The girl who was on the news?' asked Rachel, half turning to him.

'Yes, that's right.' He nodded, his face set into grim lines.

'Has she been murdered?'

'It looks like it,' he replied, 'but I'd like your opinion.' By this time they had reached the towpath. 'Watch your step here.' Nick turned and helped her to climb over a low brick wall. 'The path is very muddy after all this rain.' He looked up, narrowing his eyes against the wind and rain. 'It's about three hundred yards further on.'

In single file they made their way along the towpath, dense undergrowth to the left of them and the muddy depths of the canal to their right. On a summer's day the canal was a delightful place dividing buttercup-filled water meadows, a place where families with young children came to play or to have picnics. Now, on this grey autumn day, in the wind and rain, it was desolate and, with the implication of what might have taken place there, somehow forbidding. In the distance Rachel could see a group of figures, some in fluorescent jackets, others in plain dark clothes, and as they drew nearer she could see that an area of bushes and scrub had been cordoned off with the familiar blue and white tape used by the police and a tent-like covering had been constructed from green tarpaulins. Two uniformed officers guarded the construction while another plainclothes officer approached Nick and Rachel as they slipped and slithered their way down from the towpath.

He looked cold, wet and miserable. 'Afternoon, miss,' he said, nodding briefly at Rachel.

'This is Dr Beresford,' said Nick. Turning to Rachel, he briefly introduced the other man. 'DI Terry Payne.'

'Forensics are on their way, Guv,' said DI Payne, 'and a pathologist from the Home Office. We just need the doc here to certify the death. Oh, and the press have somehow got wind of it and are champing at the bit.'

'How did that happen?' Nick sounded annoyed.

'Search me, Guv.' The man shrugged his shoulders. 'You know what they're like—the slightest thing and they're all over the place like flies. And let's face it, this story has had national coverage.'

'We don't know yet that this is the young woman who has been missing,' said Nick tersely. 'First things first, so, Dr Beresford, if you'll come this way please.'

No longer was it Rachel and Nick—formalities now prevailed, and at least in front of his staff it was 'Dr Beresford' and 'DCI Kowalski'.

Nick entered the tent first then held back the flap of canvas for Rachel to do likewise.

The body lying on the ground and covered with a sheet was indeed that of a young woman and as Rachel drew back the sheet she saw that the body was naked apart from a flimsy black sequinned top. The girl's long blonde hair was wet and matted and her features appeared bloated, her lips blue. Carefully Rachel carried out the necessary tests for signs of life and briefly examined the body.

'Any observations on cause of death, Doctor?' asked Nick as Rachel straightened up.

'I would say she's been sexually assaulted and strangled,' Rachel replied. Pointing to an area of bruising on the girl's neck, she added, 'See here, these marks indicate that, but you'll have to wait for the pathologist's autopsy report, of course, to be absolutely certain.'

'Any idea how long she's been dead?' asked DI Payne.

'Again, you need to wait for the report...'

'A rough guess?' urged Nick.

'A couple of days at least,' Rachel replied, looking down at the dead girl. 'What a dreadful waste, a young woman like that with her whole life before her.' She paused. 'Do you think this is the missing girl?'

'We are pretty certain it is,' Nick replied. 'The description fits.' He turned to his colleague. 'What about the family?'

'They are being informed now that a body has been found,' Terry Payne replied.

'Who are the family?' asked Rachel, turning to Nick.

'Well, we need positive identification, of course, but if this is indeed the missing girl her name is Kaylee Munns and her family live up on the Charlwood Estate.'

'Oh.' Rachel looked up sharply. 'You mean…?'

'Yes.' Nick nodded. 'Where I used to live. That's what you meant, wasn't it?'

'No, not really.' Rachel felt colour touch her cheeks. 'I was merely indicating that I knew where it was.'

A little later, after Rachel had signed the necessary forms certifying the death the forensics team arrived and Nick escorted Rachel back to her car. 'I'll go up and see the family later,' he said.

'Would you like me to come with you?' asked Rachel as she sat in the passenger seat of her car and drew off her boots.

'I was hoping you'd say that,' Nick replied. 'It's a dire business after something like this.'

'I think the Munns family is registered at the centre,' said Rachel. 'I'm pretty certain I've seen records with that name. What time would you like me to go up there?'

'Well, we'll need formal identification first.' Nick paused. 'I would think it would be some time this evening—is that OK?'

'Of course,' she replied briskly. 'I'm not going anywhere.'

'I'll phone you first then I'll pick you up.'

'There's no need…'

'It's no problem,' he said. 'I'll need to see the family anyway. Thanks for your help, Rachel—I'll see you later.'

'Yes, all right, Nick.' She nodded then watched him as he turned and walked away back across the tarmac to the police vehicles. And still it rained, heavy, relentless, driving rain that surely would wash away any clues there might have been in the surrounding area as to how that poor girl had met her death. To Rachel's experienced eye it was all but certain that she had met a violent death, something which, no doubt, in the next few hours a pathologist would confirm. And if that proved to be the case then it was down to Nick and his colleagues to find her killer. With a sigh Rachel stowed her boots and jacket in the boot of her car then slipped behind the steering-wheel and started the engine.

On her return to the centre she called Julie to the desk. 'Julie,' she said, 'is the Munns family registered with us?'

'The Charlwood Estate Munns?' asked Julie.

'Yes, that's right.'

'Yes, they are. In fact, they are registered with Dr O'Malley so they will be under your care at present. Do you want their records?'

'Yes, please.' It made life easier that she and not one of the partners was responsible for the family in question—not that any of them would have objected to her attending them at a time such as this, but it saved a lot of explaining. 'Thanks, Julie,' she said as the receptionist passed a bundle of records across the desk.

'Have they found her—Kaylee Munns?' Julie leaned across the desk conspiratorially.

'Sorry, Julie, you know I can't answer questions like that.' Rachel turned and made her way to her consulting room. Once inside she closed the door and after sitting down at her desk began to go through the records. Kaylee had been seventeen years old and her notes showed little other than the usual child ailments and mention of infantile eczema. She had also started taking the Pill at fifteen. The second set of notes were for Kaylee's mother, Donna Munns, and there was rather more information on her. Rachel learned that she was a smoker and suffered from recurrent chest infections, that she had suffered a miscarriage before Kaylee had been born and postnatal depression following the birth of Kaylee and again two years later on the birth of Kaylee's sister, Celine. There was little on Celine save that she was asthmatic and received regular prescriptions for cortiscosteroid inhalers. She, too, had recently gone on the Pill. There did not seem to be any notes for a Mr Munns and on closer examination of Donna's records Rachel found that she had been treated for depression following the break-up of her marriage six years previously. It wasn't much but it helped to outline the medical history of the family so that Rachel knew what she might be dealing with when she visited the family later that evening.

She wished now that she'd told Nick that she would meet him there—she didn't really want him picking her up from home. She wasn't sure why she felt that way but suspected when she tried to analyse her reasons that it was to do with her earlier resolve of keeping her dealings with Nick on a strictly professional basis. She didn't want any more from this man who had once meant the whole world to her and who still, after all this time, had the power to make her heart leap at the sight of him, or to make her knees go weak at the sound of his voice. He had hurt her badly then, had let her down when she had fondly believed that he thought as much of her as she did of him. And there was no guarantee that given half a chance he wouldn't do the same thing again. She knew if she had any sense at all she would be well advised to keep him at arm's length.

So why was it that, on her return home that evening, she was on edge waiting for the phone to ring, waiting for Nick to tell her that he would shortly be picking her up? At last when the phone did ring and she grabbed it, once again, as on that previous occasion, the caller remained silent before hanging up. She gazed at the phone in exasperation then dialled the number to find out who had called, only to be told that the caller had withheld their number. Slowly she replaced the handset. It was the second time that had happened but, she reasoned, it could be someone trying to contact the owners of St Edmund's, not realising they were away. Not that that should prevent them from speaking. It was irritating to say the least but not something that she could do much about.

When the phone did ring again she answered it in some trepidation, once again to find that it wasn't Nick on the other end of the line.

'Jeremy!' she exclaimed, not sure whether she was pleased or annoyed to hear from him at that particular moment.

'Was just wondering how you are,' he said.

'I'm fine, Jeremy, fine—how are you?'

'Yes, pretty good,' he replied. 'Everything is much the same here. So how are you finding Westhampstead? Has it changed much from how you remember it?'

'In some ways, yes, in others not at all,' she said. 'But it's been nice to catch up with old friends. Listen, Jeremy, did you ring just now—about half an hour ago?'

'No,' he replied. 'Why?'

'Oh, no reason really. Someone rang and didn't leave their number, that's all.'

'Annoying, that,' he said, 'but, no, it wasn't me. I've only just come in and I thought I'd give you a ring, have a chat, see how you're getting on, that sort of thing.'

'That's nice.' She paused. 'But actually, Jeremy, do

you think we could talk at some other time? I could ring you back later tonight if you like, otherwise maybe to-morrow evening. You see—'

'Going out on the town, are you?'

'No,' she said quickly, 'well, yes, I am going out, but not on the town. I have to go out on police business— I'm waiting for a call now to give me details.'

'So you're still involved in police work, then?'

'Yes, the partner I've taken over from was police doc-tor for this area and as I was involved in that sort of work before, it seemed logical. Besides, I enjoy it.'

'Wouldn't do for me,' said Jeremy. 'All those night call outs just to deal with a bunch of drunks.'

'It isn't all like that,' Rachel protested. 'Some of the cases are very interesting.'

'What's tonight's excitement, then?'

'I'm sorry?'

'Didn't you just say you were going out on police business tonight?'

'Oh. Yes.' She hesitated then decided it was probably all right to talk to a fellow doctor. 'A body was found this afternoon. I was called to certify the death.'

'Suspicious circumstances, was it?'

'It looks like it, yes.'

'So what do you have to do tonight?'

'I'm visiting the girl's family.'

'Rather you than me.'

Suddenly she could picture Jeremy's expression and for some reason the image irritated her. 'Yes, well,' she said briskly, 'someone has to do it.'

'Just make sure you take care if there's some sort of nutter at large.'

'Oh, I'll be all right,' she said quickly. 'The local DCI is picking me up and taking me to the house.'

'Very obliging of him—do they usually do that?'

'Er, no, not really.' She swallowed. 'I happen to know him, so I expect that's got something to do with it. But I really must go. Shall I ring you back later?'

'If you like,' he replied. 'I'll probably be here. Bye, now.'

'Bye, Jeremy.' She hung up, wondering what Jeremy was thinking, but there was little time for much speculation for almost immediately her doorbell rang and she hurried into the hall to answer it. Tugging open the door, she found Nick on the doorstep and her heart did its usual gymnastics.

'Nick…you were going to ring…'

'Your phone was engaged,' he said, stepping into the hall and shutting the door behind him, 'and your mobile was switched off.'

'Sorry,' she said breathlessly. 'I won't keep you a minute. I'll just get a coat…'

'Do you make a habit of doing that?' he asked as she turned from the hall cupboard after retrieving a coat.

'What?' She frowned, wondering to what he was referring.

'Opening the door after dark when you don't know who's there.'

'Well…no, actually, I don't.' Suddenly she felt flustered, as if he'd caught her out in some serious misdemeanour. 'I usually have the door on the chain.'

'But tonight you didn't?' he said coolly.

'No,' she agreed, 'tonight I didn't.'

'That's all it takes, Rachel.'

'I know, I know—I'll take more care in future.'

'You must,' he said grimly, 'especially now.'

Rachel was struggling into her coat but she paused

and looked at him. 'Have you had the pathologist's report yet?'

'No, not yet.' He stepped forward to help her, easing her coat over her shoulders. 'But I would say it's pretty much a foregone conclusion, wouldn't you? The semi-naked body of a young girl is found and there are signs of violence and sexual assault.'

Rachel gave an involuntary little shiver. 'Have you had formal identification yet?'

'Yes.' He opened the front door. 'It is Kaylee Munns, so the sooner we get up to see her family the better.'

The rain had subsided to a light drizzle as Rachel and Nick left the house and in Nick's dark saloon drove out of Cathedral Close and joined the main road that ran through the centre of town.

'That's a nice house you have there,' he commented as he drove.

'Oh, it isn't mine,' said Rachel quickly. 'I'm only renting it. It belongs to friends of my parents—they are abroad at the moment. But you're right, it is a nice house. In fact, it's so nice I won't want to leave it when my year is up.'

'So what will you do when your year is up?' He spoke lightly but Rachel detected a slight edge to his voice.

'I'm not sure really, go back to Stockport probably.'

'And to Jeremy?'

'Yes…probably.'

'You don't sound very sure.'

She shrugged and gazed out of the window at the lighted windows of the high street shops. She didn't want to talk about Jeremy and what might happen if she returned to Stockport—somehow she couldn't even visualise it.

'Was it Jeremy you were talking to?'

'I'm sorry?' She turned her head and looked at his profile, that same profile she had once never tired of gazing at.

'When I was trying to get through to you and your phone was engaged?'

'Oh, that,' she said. 'Yes, that was Jeremy.'

'Missing you, is he?'

'I don't know,' she replied truthfully. 'He didn't really say.'

'I'm amazed he's let you come,' he said after a moment. 'There aren't many men who would let their woman out of their sight for a whole year.'

'Maybe not.' She shrugged again. 'But like I said, this year is meant to be a testing time—a trial separation, if you like,' she added with a touch of desperation, wanting him to understand but not knowing why it should matter so much to her that he should.

He gave a short laugh. 'In my book, there's no such thing,' he said. 'When couples start talking of trial separations it means one thing. As far as I'm concerned, it simply prolongs the agony.'

'So you're of the clean-break brigade?' she asked coolly. 'Is that what you're saying?'

'Absolutely,' he replied.

Yes, she thought bitterly, staring ahead and becoming mesmerised by the steady sweep of the windscreen wipers, that's what you did to me.

They were silent for a while as Nick negotiated the car round a series of roundabouts then took the Charlwood exit. 'Does he know about me?' he asked a little later.

Instinctively Rachel knew he was referring to their past relationship and not their current acquaintance. 'I may have mentioned you.' Rachel swallowed. 'Yes, now

I think about it, I did tell him that there was once some-one from home…'

'Is that all I'd become—someone from home?' There was real bitterness in his tone now and it stung Rachel to a sharp retort.

'Well, I doubt you talked much to Marilyn about me,' she said, 'apart from being someone you once knew.'

'It was a bit different with Marilyn,' he replied tersely.

'Oh? And why was that?' She could barely keep the sarcasm from her voice.

'Marilyn knew you and she knew all about us.'

'How did she know about us?' Rachel frowned in the darkness.

'Our mothers were friends, neighbours,' he replied. 'Marilyn was always in our house when we were grow-ing up. She might have seen you, or, if not, my mother would have told her mother about you.'

Silently Rachel digested that particular piece of infor-mation, trying to remember if Marilyn Rooney had in-deed been around when she had visited Nick's home. 'Did she always have a crush on you?' she asked curi-ously at last.

'So I'm told.' He paused. 'She always thought you'd taken me away from her.'

'And had I?' She turned and stared at him again. She couldn't see his features in the darkness but she sensed the way his jaw had tightened.

'Of course not,' he retorted. 'Marilyn may have had a crush on me in those days, but she was just a kid. I never started seeing her until long after you and I—'

'But there were others,' she said quickly. 'After me, I mean.'

'What makes you think that?'

'One hears these things.' She shrugged again, remembering the pain she'd felt when her mother had told her about various girls Nick had been seen with.

'Well, maybe there were,' he said, 'but, as we've already said, it was all a long time ago.'

By this time they had reached the vast Charlwood Estate, which covered many acres of land to the east of Westhampstead. Nick drove in silence past rows of houses and tenement blocks and a lighted shopping mall where groups of youths loitered outside and young boys played on skateboards.

'It seems strange to be up here again,' said Rachel as the road wound round to the left and they drove past the house where Nick had lived as a boy with his family. 'Do any of your family still live here?'

'No.' He shook his head. 'There was only my sister after Mum died and she's now married and living in London.' He paused then went on, 'Now, we want Greystone Avenue and, if my memory serves me right, that is over here…' He turned and after driving for about a hundred yards they saw two police vehicles parked beneath a streetlight outside a row of terraced houses. 'That's it,' he said drawing up behind the cars. 'Number 86.'

He switched off the engine and glanced at Rachel. 'Are you ready for this?' he asked quietly. 'It could be pretty harrowing.'

'Nick, I'm a doctor,' she said firmly.

'Yes,' he said, 'I know. I'm sorry. I guess I still thought you needed protecting.'

'Come on, let's get on with it. It won't be pleasant but that's what we're here for.'

Together, they climbed out of the car and walked towards the house.

CHAPTER FOUR

THE door was opened by a uniformed police officer who showed Nick and Rachel into the family living room where a woman and a young girl were huddled together on a settee. A WPC was sitting beside them while a man, who could have been anywhere in age from thirty to forty, paced the room, turning as they entered, one hand at the back of his neck in a gesture that suggested helplessness. The woman on the settee looked haggard from lack of sleep and red-eyed with weeping. The girl was sobbing uncontrollably.

'Mrs Munns—Donna.' Nick crouched in front of the two as the WPC stood up and moved away. As Donna looked up, he went on, 'I'm Detective Chief Inspector Kowalski and this is Dr Beresford from the Westhampstead group practice.'

The dull expression in Donna Munns's eyes suggested that there was no one who could help her now because the worst had happened.

'Hello, Donna, hello, Celine,' said Rachel gently, glancing from the older woman to the girl at her side. 'I'm so very sorry to hear about Kaylee and I know there isn't much I can say that will be of any help. Your own doctor, Dr O'Malley, is away at the moment, so that's why—'

'She only went to a club for the evening.' Donna interrupted Rachel in mid-sentence and her expression was as if she hadn't heard a word the doctor had said. 'She had a new sparkly top to wear,' she went on in the same flat tone. 'I told her not to be late. She laughed and told me that I worry too much, that…that she'd be all right… Oh, God!' She put one hand, which shook uncontrollably, over her mouth as if what had happened was only just beginning to sink in.

'I'm going to prescribe something for you to help you through this,' said Rachel, sitting back on her heels on the floor, opening her case and taking out a prescription pad. While she was writing a prescription for sedatives she realised that Nick was talking in low tones to the man, who had now ceased his pacing and was staring out of the window through a narrow opening in the drawn curtains.

'And what was she doing on the towpath?' Donna carried on talking, half to herself and half to anyone who might be listening. 'She would never have come home that way in the dark—not in a million years she wouldn't…'

At that moment the door opened and a policeman came into the room and indicated for Nick to join him outside. Rachel tore the form off the prescription pad and handed it to the WPC. 'Is there someone who will fetch this from the chemist?' she asked.

'Yes, Mrs Munns's sister and her husband are here,' the policewoman replied, then lowering her voice so that only Rachel could hear, she added, 'They identified the body.' As if to endorse her words Nick came back into the room accompanied by a woman who bore a strong resemblance to Donna. The woman, tears pouring down her own face, went straight to the settee and sat between her sister and her niece, putting an arm around each of them.

Nick looked grim-faced. Glancing first at the man by the window then directly at Donna, he said, 'I'm sorry but there's no easy way of telling you this but you have to know. I have just received the pathologist's report and it confirms that your daughter was, in fact, murdered. There will now, of course, be a complete and thorough police investigation into her death.'

'You were right.' Nick threw Rachel a sidelong glance. 'Kaylee was strangled and there was evidence that she was also raped.' It was some time later and Rachel was seated beside Nick in his car while he drove her back to Cathedral Close.

'That was gruelling up there at the Munns' house,' said Rachel, taking a deep breath and momentarily leaning back against the headrest and closing her eyes. 'That poor family. Honestly, I don't know how anyone recovers from something like this.'

'I think it's pretty fair to say they don't,' Nick replied, 'not really. But, then, you wouldn't, would you, not if it was a member of your own family?'

'No, I suppose not.' Rachel opened her eyes and stared ahead at the wet road surface shining in the light from the car's headlights.

'I know I wouldn't if it was Lucy,' said Nick quietly, 'or if it had been my mother or my sister.'

'What happens next?' asked Rachel. 'For you, I mean?'

'I go back to headquarters and assemble my investigation team,' he replied. 'I've already had a call from my superintendent asking me to head the inquiry—we then set up an incident room and start collecting information.'

'Any thoughts yet?' Rachel turned her head but the sight of that uncompromising profile did something to her insides and she turned back.

'I try to keep an open mind at this stage,' he replied tersely.

They were silent for a while then Rachel spoke. 'Do we know if Kaylee had a boyfriend, or whether she went to the club alone?'

'She did have a boyfriend, apparently,' Nick replied, 'but according to her sister they split up a couple of weeks ago.'

'So presumably he'll be questioned?'

'Of course.' Nick inhaled sharply. 'As will the group of girls she was with at the club that night.'

'Did the pathology say whether she was killed where she was found?'

'They thought she had been killed elsewhere and her body taken there and dumped.'

'Thus endorsing Donna Munns's theory that her daughter would never have walked home alone along the towpath.'

'Unless, of course, she wasn't alone, but we need to wait for forensics to report before we can reach any firm conclusions on that.'

'Who was the guy at the house?' asked Rachel after a moment.

'Donna Munns's boyfriend, apparently,' Nick replied. 'The girls' father left home years ago and I understand this is Donna's second live-in boyfriend.'

'A possible suspect?'

'He'll be questioned, certainly,' Nick replied, 'as will anyone else in any way connected with the Munns family, which includes the uncle who identified the body. But it's very easy to jump to conclusions in these cases, especially when there is a stereotypical suspect—so, like I said, I like to keep an open mind.' He paused as the car drew into Cathedral Close and came to a stop before

St Edmund's. 'Here we are,' he said, 'home safe and sound. Thanks for your help, Rachel.'

'Don't mention it. I didn't feel I could do very much.'

'You'd be surprised,' he replied, his voice softening. 'The presence of a GP in these situations can be very reassuring for the family.'

'I may call again to see them—if that's all right?' She threw him a quick glance.

'Yes, of course.' He nodded. 'Anything that will help. Well, I guess I'd better get on down to headquarters—I have a feeling this is going to be a long night.'

For a moment there was an awkward silence between them and just for one wild instant Rachel had to fight the absurd urge to lean over and kiss him goodnight. She would have done so once, unhesitatingly, but the barrier of time prevented that, now making it unthinkable. With a murmured goodnight she opened the car door and got out, her feet slithering on the wet pavement. Before she had a chance to shut the door Nick leaned towards her, lowering his head. 'Don't forget, will you,' he said, 'what I told you?'

'What you told me?' She frowned, wondering what he meant.

'Yes, about opening the door to strangers.'

'Oh, that.' She smiled.

'Yes, that.' He was deadly serious. 'Keep the chain on the door. There's a killer out there, Rachel.'

A sudden shiver ran down her spine. 'Most murders are by someone known to the victim,' she said lightly.

'That's as may be,' he gave a slight shrug, 'but it doesn't mean you shouldn't take care.'

'All right.' She smiled again. 'Goodnight, Nick.'

'Goodnight, Rachel.'

She shut the car door and stood back before realising

that he was waiting for her to go into the house. Fumbling slightly, she took the keys out of her pocket, unlocked the door, opened it and switched on the lights. Only then did Nick lift one hand and draw away. Rachel watched the tail lights of his car as it disappeared out of the close, then with a little sigh she closed the door, bolted it and secured the chain.

The town of Westhampstead was abuzz with the news of Kaylee Munns's murder. Groups of people congregated in the most unlikely places to discuss the events of the last few days, not least of these being the staff-room of the medical centre.

'I can hardly believe it,' said Julie as she, Rachel, practice nurse Patti Roberts and partner Dr Bruce Mitchell lingered over morning coffee. 'I can't ever remember a murder in Westhamstead before.'

'There was one once, a long time ago,' mused Bruce. 'I don't remember all the details but it was a woman who was murdered in a farmhouse just off the M4.'

'Did they catch who did it?' asked Patti.

'Yes.' Bruce screwed up his face in concentration. 'If I remember rightly it was her husband. I think she'd been having an affair and he'd caught her with her lover or something like that. Anyway, he got a life sentence.'

'I hope they catch this one soon,' said Julie with a shiver. 'Honestly, it's not safe to go out on your own.'

'Folk don't seem to be able to talk about anything else,' said Patti.

'That's true,' Rachel agreed, recalling how almost every one of her patients in that morning's surgery had mentioned the murder.

'I wonder if the police have anyone in mind,' mused Bruce as he drained his cup and stood up, collecting up

a variety of records, medical journals and repeat prescription forms.

'Do you know if they have a suspect, Rachel?' asked
Patti. 'What with you being involved at the station.'

'No, I'm afraid they don't volunteer that sort of information to me,' said Rachel. 'Although, from what I
have heard, all police leave has been cancelled while the
enquiries are going on.'

'They were doing house-to-house enquiries up on the
Charlwood Estate,' said Julie. 'Philip's mum lives up
there and she said they called on her—not that she could
tell them anything, of course. She's elderly and hardly
goes out these days.'

'I must get on,' said Rachel as she, too, stood up. As
Bruce and Patti left the room and she started to follow
them, Julie called her back.

'Rachel,' she said, and Rachel paused, one hand on
the doorhandle, and looked back.

'Yes?' she said.

'Could I book myself in to see you this afternoon?'

'To see me?' Rachel hesitated. 'Aren't you registered
with Dr Davenport?'

'Yes, I am, but he doesn't have any free appointments
for a few days and, well, actually, it's something I would
really rather discuss with a woman.'

'All right. Put yourself in wherever there's a space.'

'Thanks, Rachel.' Julie smiled.

By the time Rachel received the afternoon's surgery list
it was full, and after casting her eye down the list Rachel
saw that Julie had put herself in about halfway down.

She worked steadily through the list, dealing with the
usual variety of patients, from a baby with teething dif-

ficulties to an elderly man with prostate problems, a woman suffering badly from menopausal mood swings to a child with an ear infection. As the little boy and his mother left the room Julie tapped on the door and came in. Rachel was surprised to see that her husband Philip accompanied her. From what Julie had said, Rachel had imagined she wanted a confidential chat about some intimate ailment.

'Julie, Philip.' She looked from one to the other— Julie with her dark hair and olive complexion, and, in complete contrast, Philip with his red hair and white skin. 'Please, come in and sit down.' When they were both seated, she said, 'Now, how may I help you?'

'We want to see about IVF treatment.' It was Philip who answered.

'I see' said Rachel. 'So, tell me, have you been trying for a family for very long?'

'Ages,' said Philip.

'Not really,' said Julie. Glancing at Philip, she added, 'It hasn't really been that long, Philip.' She turned back to Rachel. 'We used precautions for a long time because we couldn't really afford to start a family.'

'I see from your notes, Julie, that you were taking an oral contraceptive,' said Rachel, studying Julie's medication chart on her computer screen. 'So when did you come off the Pill?'

'About a year ago.'

'It should have happened in a year,' said Philip.

'Not necessarily,' Rachel replied. 'Sometimes it takes longer than that for a woman's body to get back to normal after taking oral contraceptives. I would like to examine you, Julie, but I think it's far too soon to be talking about IVF treatment. If you'd just like to slip into my examination room and undress, I'll be with you in a moment.' Julie stood up and walked through the communicating door into the examination room.

'So you don't think there is too much of a problem, then?' said Philip, leaning forward earnestly.

'I wouldn't think so,' Rachel replied. 'But let's wait and see, shall we?' In an attempt to lighten the atmosphere while they waited for Julie to undress, she said, 'Did you sell all your raffle tickets, Philip?'

'Nearly.' He nodded.

'When does the draw take place?'

'At the Michaelmas Fair at the end of the month,' he replied.

'Heavens,' she said, 'I'd forgotten all about the Michaelmas Fairs. I didn't realise they still held them. We all used to go to them in the old days, didn't we?'

He nodded. 'Some of us still do,' he said, his face breaking into a grin. 'Maybe you'll join us again this year.'

'Maybe I will at that.' Rachel smiled then stood up and walked across to the examination room.

A little later, after examining Julie thoroughly and questioning her at some length about her monthly periods and the regularity of her cycle, Rachel rejoined Philip who looked up expectantly. 'We'll just wait for Julie,' she said, crossing to the basin to wash her hands. By the time she had finished Julie had dressed and rejoined them.

Rachel came straight to the point as Julie sat down. 'I will write a referral to a gynaecologist. I think, Julie, there may be a chance from what you have told me that you could be suffering from a condition called endometriosis.'

'That can result in blocked Fallopian tubes, can't it?' Julie looked alarmed.

'Let's not jump to any conclusions,' said Rachel. 'A specialist will carry out the necessary tests and be able to tell you more.'

She spent the next five minutes trying to reassure Julie and Philip that even if Julie did have endometriosis it didn't necessarily mean they couldn't start a family but that they would have to wait and see what the test results showed.

After the Newtons had gone Rachel carried on with her list then discovered that the last person that afternoon was Tommy Page. Her heart sank when Tommy came into the room and there was no sign of his mother, Eileen. 'Hello, Tommy,' she said. 'All on your own to-day?'

'Mum's gone shopping,' said Tommy, coming right into the room and sitting down. He was wearing a navy-blue tracksuit with what appeared to be a red football shirt.

'Does she know you've come to see me, Tommy?' asked Rachel warily.

'No.' Tommy giggled and slowly shook his head. 'I made an appointment,' he said, 'all by myself.'

'So why did you want to see me, Tommy?' asked Rachel when he fell silent again.

'Because...I like you,' he said simply. 'I wanted to see you.'

'Well, that's very nice, Tommy,' she said, 'but really, you know, you should only come here to the surgery to see me if you've got something wrong with you—if you aren't very well,' she added, when he didn't appear to have grasped what she meant.

He frowned and appeared to be concentrating intently, then he said, 'I could come and see you at your house.'

'I don't think that would be a very good idea,' said

Rachel. She was about to say that he didn't know where she lived but thought better of it, imagining that he might demand to be told.

'Why not?' he said.

'Well, it just wouldn't,' she said. 'Now, Tommy—'

'I know where you live,' he said. 'You live near the big church. Mum showed me where you live.'

Rachel took a deep breath, knowing she had to stop this. 'Tommy,' she said firmly, 'if you don't have anything wrong with you today, I'm afraid you'll have to go so that I can see people who do have things wrong with them.'

'No more people out there,' he said. 'I'm the last one.'

'Even so…'

'I've got tummyache,' he said, 'right here.' He pointed to his stomach.

Rachel was on the point of calling another member of staff in to chaperone while she examined Tommy when, quite suddenly, he stood up and turned to the door. 'I'll come back tomorrow with Mum,' he said. Opening the door, he ambled off into the corridor.

With a deep sigh Rachel sank back into her chair, then after a moment's reflection she pressed the intercom. 'Danielle?' she said when the receptionist answered. 'In future I can only see Tommy Page if his mother is with him.'

'Sorry,' said Danielle. 'We did wonder about that. He's never come on his own before.'

Tommy didn't come back to see Rachel the following day but towards the end of her morning surgery something happened that in a way was far more disturbing. It was between patients when she was entering a report onto the computer that she saw that she had incoming email. There were two messages—the first from a pharmaceutical company, advertising a new brand of anti-inflammatory drugs, and the second which had no subject and came from someone listed as 'your friend'. When she opened it the message simply said: *I really do love you Rachel.*

She stared at it. Surely this couldn't be from Tommy Page, not through email? Then she remembered that Eileen had told her that the day centre Tommy attended had fixed him up with his own computer. It had to be from Tommy, just as the handwritten note had been, although heaven only knew how he had obtained her email address.

Really, she thought, she should tell someone about this. But at the same time Tommy was harmless and she didn't want to get him into any sort of trouble. The poor man had obviously developed a crush on her and provided it didn't go any further she felt she could cope with it. She had already told the staff she wouldn't see him alone again and apart from that, there had only been the note and this.

Suddenly she remembered the phone calls, the ones where the caller had hung up when she'd answered and had withheld their number, but she doubted those had been anything to do with Tommy. That sort of thing happened all the time—wrong numbers, or someone hanging up without speaking. No, she really didn't think she needed to do anything about this. Purposefully she deleted the email and pressed the buzzer for her next patient.

She had almost finished her surgery when Danielle buzzed through to tell her that the police were on the line, wanting to speak to her.

'Thank you, Danielle. Put them through.' Her pulse

had started to race but she took a deep breath, steadying herself as she waited to hear Nick's voice.

'Dr Beresford?' She felt a stab of disappointment. 'Sergeant Mason here.'

'Hello, Sergeant,' she said briskly. 'How may I help you?'

'We have rather an unusual case, Doctor, which we'd like you to take a look at if you will.'

'Of course.' She tried to sound matter-of-fact and efficient but her heart had started hammering again at the thought of going to the station—with the murder investigations that were going on there was a very good chance that Nick would be there. 'Can you give me any details over the phone, in case the patient is registered here and I'm able to bring any records with me?'

'I doubt she's registered anywhere,' Harry Mason replied. 'It's a woman called Maisie Trott, she's homeless. I'm sure you must have seen her around the town,' he went on. 'Sometimes she sits in the precinct, sometimes she sits down near the canal. She's always surrounded by plastic carrier bags bulging with rags. Every so often she causes a disturbance, knowing full well she will be brought in here and will have a meal and a night in the cells. Anyway, the disturbance happened this morning but I'm a bit concerned about Maisie. She simply isn't her usual self.'

'Can you describe any symptoms?' asked Rachel, making notes on a pad.

'She's very lethargic,' Harry said. 'She's also slurring her words and her movements are very uncoordinated. She just isn't herself.'

'OK. I'll come down and have a look at her,' said Rachel. 'I should be with you in twenty minutes or so.'

Moments later she leaned across the reception desk.

'Danielle,' she said, 'I have a police call out. I'm not sure how long I'll be but I should be back for afternoon surgery.'

She hurried out to her car then took a moment before switching on the engine, resting her hands on the steering-wheel in an attempt to calm herself. This heightened sense of excitement whenever there was any chance of seeing Nick really would have to stop. She knew that it was utterly ridiculous and quite pathetic. Here she was, a grown woman, a professional, a doctor, and she was behaving in exactly the same way as she had when she and Nick had been in their teens. It was crazy—they had both moved on in the intervening years, built their careers. Nick had even married and was a father, for heaven's sake. No doubt he'd be horrified if he knew how she was feeling and, besides, she had Jeremy, didn't she? Lukewarm as that particular relationship had become, Jeremy was still to all intents and purposes very much on the scene.

Taking a deep breath, she started the car. She really would have to get to grips with this situation and get herself firmly under control again.

But just supposing—the thought, unbidden, crept into her mind as she drove out of the car park into the golden-leafed avenue—Nick also had been affected at seeing her again? He was divorced, supposedly a free agent these days unless there was something he hadn't told her, so what would she do if he were to ask her out?

She should refuse him, she knew that. He had been wholly unsuitable in the past and there was no reason to suppose that he was any different now in spite of his status in the force. There had always been an element of the dangerous about Nick Kowalski, the sort of danger that prompted parents to lock up their daughters, and Rachel doubted that sort of thing ever changed.

But just supposing she ignored all that and agreed to go out with him again. What then? What sort of footing would their relationship be on? Would he expect to carry on where they had left off all those years ago? Rachel squirmed in her seat as images of hot summer nights full of passion slipped into her mind. He couldn't expect that, surely? And she wouldn't want that again, would she?

Not under any circumstances, she told herself firmly as she drove through the town.

She was greeted in the reception area of police head-quarters by Harry Mason who, without further ado, con-ducted her to a cell where Maisie Trott was sitting on the single bed, surrounded by her bags and possessions. She looked to Rachel to be somewhere between sixty-five and seventy, with wild, unkempt, matted grey hair, a florid complexion, which suggested possible abuse of alcohol, and bowed legs, which might or might not have been due to childhood rickets. There had been no records for Maisie at the medical centre but before they reached the cell Harry had explained to Rachel that in the past, with the exception of the odd night in the cells, which usually coincided with an onset of colder weather, Maisie had refused all offers of help from Social Services but grudgingly accepted small gestures from the Salvation Army.

'Hello, Maisie.' Rachel crouched in front of the woman, aware as she did so of an almost overpowering smell that emanated from her unwashed person and many layers of clothing. Her face appeared curiously lopsided and the skin around her mouth seemed stretched into an almost permanent inane smile, but that was where it ended, for her eyes were vacant and devoid of any emotion. She appeared not to have seen Rachel, or, if she had, chose to ignore her. Carefully, with the assistance of a WPC who helped to remove some of Maisie's clothing, Rachel managed to carry out an examination, checking pulse, blood pressure and blood sugar and sounding Maisie's heart and lungs.

When she had finished she left the WPC to help Maisie to replace her clothing and went to report to Harry.

'What's wrong with her?' asked Harry, looking up from the desk.

'I'm pretty certain she's suffered a mild stroke,' Rachel replied. 'I'd like her transferred to hospital for assessment, so could you send for an ambulance, please?'

'She'll hate that,' said Harry, picking up the phone.

'There's no way she's going to be able to carry on as she has, sleeping rough and living on the streets,' said Rachel. 'Do we know anything else about her? For instance, does she have any family?'

'Does who have any family?' said an all-too-familiar voice behind her, and as Rachel turned her head she found Nick at her elbow. He looked tired but impossibly handsome in a black leather jacket, roll-neck shirt and moleskin trousers. She swallowed and looked away. 'Maisie Trott,' she said quickly in reply to his question.

'Poor old Maisie—what's she done now?' asked Nick.

'She hasn't really done anything,' Harry replied. 'She was picked up in the precinct and at first we just thought it was the usual—you know, Maisie causing a rumpus in order to get a night in the cells—but she didn't seem too good when she came in so I called the doc here.'

'I think she's suffered a stroke,' Rachel went on.

'We're transferring her to hospital. I was just asking if you know anything about Maisie's family.'

'We don't know much about her at all,' said Harry. 'There's always a lot of speculation about someone like Maisie, but it's sometimes difficult to sort out fact from rumour.'

'I understood she came from a wealthy family who paid her to stay away,' said Nick. 'But, like you say, that could simply be part of the myth. She'll hate hospital, won't she, Harry?'

'That's what I was saying to the doctor,' Harry replied. 'But this time I don't think she'll have a lot of choice.'

'She'll certainly have to go somewhere where she can be looked after,' said Rachel. Then, as Harry began talking to someone at Ambulance Control, she turned to Nick again. 'How is the investigation going?' she asked.

'If you're finished here,' he said, his steady gaze meeting hers, 'why don't you come along to the incident room and see for yourself?'

'All right.' Trying to ignore the fact that yet again her heart was beating faster than it usually did, she raised one hand to Harry then followed Nick out of Reception and down a long corridor to the rear of the building.

The incident room was abuzz with activity, with at least a dozen police personnel either answering phones or seated at computer screens feeding in information. A huge board had been set up at one end of the room and was covered with information, which appeared to include autopsy photographs of the dead girl and a large-scale map of the area covered with coloured pins.

'We've had an overwhelming response from the public,' said Nick as he stood beside Rachel and surveyed the room. 'All that information, of course, has to be sifted through and collated and any possible leads followed up.' He paused as DI Terry Payne stood up from behind a desk and crossed the room to join them.

'Terry?' he said expectantly.

'Guv, Doc.' Terry acknowledged Nick and Rachel, then shook his head. 'No,' he went on, 'nothing with that one. The guy was in London at the time and there are plenty to vouch for him.'

'Right, Terry. Carry on.' Nick drew a deep breath. 'Come to my office,' he said briefly to Rachel. 'It's a bit quieter in there. Unless…' He paused. 'Are you in much of a hurry to get back?'

Rachel glanced at her watch. 'I have to be back for afternoon surgery at two but I'm OK till then.'

'In that case,' said Nick decisively, 'I'll send out for coffee and sandwiches if you'd care to join me for lunch. It's not exactly the Ritz but I'm afraid it's the best we can do.'

'Sounds fine to me.' Rachel spoke casually with a deliberate attempt at nonchalance, which belied her inner turmoil, a turmoil that told her that, in spite of her earlier resolve to the contrary, she would have been happy to join Nick for lunch wherever the venue and whatever the circumstances.

CHAPTER FIVE

'WAS that line of enquiry a dead end?' asked Rachel as she sat down on the chair that Nick indicated.

He nodded. 'Yes, it was Kaylee's previous boyfriend.'

'The one she'd just finished with?'

'That's the one.' Nick replied. 'Obviously we wanted to question him but, as you heard Terry say, he was in London at the time and it sounds like he has a strong alibi.'

'Do you have any other strong suspects?' asked Rachel. 'What about the members of Kaylee's family?'

'Well, her mother's boyfriend has a good alibi—he was in the local pub for the entire evening that Kaylee went missing, together with her mother and a whole bunch of locals who can vouch for them. When they left the pub they went home, watched television for a while then went to bed.'

'So when did they report Kaylee missing?' asked Rachel.

'Apparently, Donna woke up at three-thirty and went to the bathroom—it was then that she realised that Kaylee hadn't come home. She rang a friend of Kaylee's who told her that Kaylee had left the club early—before midnight, in fact. It was then that Donna reported her daughter missing.'

'And you don't have any other leads?'

Nick ran one hand over his head in a futile gesture and suddenly Rachel felt sorry for him, with the intense pressure he was under. 'Not really,' he admitted. 'I know we said we've had a good response from the public but I'm afraid most of it is pure speculation. However, there may be just one nugget of truth there so it all has to be examined, every lead has to be followed up.'

'Was it usual for Kaylee to leave the club before her friends?' asked Rachel thoughtfully.

'Apparently not,' Nick replied. 'Most of her friends hadn't even realised she'd gone, except for the one who actually saw her go just before midnight. Needless to say, we've questioned the girl thoroughly. She's pretty distraught but she did manage to tell us that she'd seen Kaylee on the club dance floor earlier in the evening, dancing with a guy she—the girl—didn't know. The only thing she was really able to remember about him was that he wasn't wearing a shirt and that he wore a red bandana around his head.'

'So no doubt you're wanting to speak to the man in the red bandana,' said Rachel, looking up as a young constable arrived with coffee and sandwiches.

'Quite,' Nick replied briefly. Taking the tray from the constable, he thanked him then set it down on the desk between them. 'We've studied CCTV footage of that night at the club with Kaylee's friend but we weren't able to identify either Kaylee or the red bandana man. No one else at the club that night has any recollection of him.'

'Is there a drug problem at the club?' asked Rachel.

'Unfortunately, yes.' Nick scowled into his coffee, as if having to admit to a drug problem on his patch was in some way a reflection on the efficiency of his force. 'We have an ongoing investigation but, yes, there are dealers supplying ecstasy and other drugs to local kids.'

'How Westhampstead has changed,' said Rachel, peeling the Cellophane from a packet of sandwiches.

'There was nothing like that when we were kids.' She paused and looked up when Nick remained silent. 'Was there?' she said.

He shrugged. 'Probably in certain areas but not anywhere where nicely brought-up young ladies went.'

'Do you think this particular case has anything to do with drugs?' asked Rachel, ignoring his reference to what he had always seen as her privileged upbringing.

Nick shook his head. 'No, actually, I don't. Kaylee wasn't a known drug user. According to her friends she'd tried ecstasy once but it made her feel so ill she never touched anything again, and there was no evidence of drugs in her body from the pathologist's report. Red bandana man may have been a pusher, he may have been Kaylee's killer, he may have been both, but until we find him we can only speculate.'

'Do you have any theories of your own—even if they are unsubstantiated?' asked Rachel thoughtfully as she took a mouthful of coffee that, somewhat surprisingly, really was very good.

Nick shrugged, 'For what it's worth, I think Kaylee may have simply been in the wrong place at the wrong time. The killer was on the prowl, maybe saw her in the club, or as she left the club alone, and followed her. According to the pathologist she put up a real fight.'

'I would second that,' Rachel replied. 'And the time of death is estimated at about twelve-thirty, which does suggest that she was killed shortly after she left the club.'

'That's right. We think the killer then took her body, probably in the boot of a car, down to Millar's Wharf, carried it along the towpath and dumped it in the undergrowth.'

'So we are talking about someone strong,' Rachel mused. 'That would have been some weight to carry.'

'True,' Nick agreed, 'although it's only a short distance. The thing is, no one seems to have noticed anything untoward that night—a struggle in the vicinity of the club or any unusual goings-on at Millar's Wharf.'

'There must be someone, somewhere who saw something,' said Rachel firmly.

'Yes, I know, that's why we need to go back and re-examine the facts and keep on doing that until we get some sort of breakthrough. The BBC is going to do a reconstruction on their crime programme in the hope that it will jog someone's memory.'

'In the meantime, there's no let-up for you. You look tired, Nick,' she said, leaning forward slightly and looking into his face.

'It goes with the territory—I'm used to it.'

'Even so, there's no point in going for burn-out—that way you'll be no use to anyone. Are you not getting any time off at all?'

'Well, all leave has been cancelled...'

'I know that,' she replied, 'but even you must have a day off eventually. This could go on for weeks.'

'Hell, I hope not.' He passed one hand over his head. 'The superintendent is breathing down my neck as it is...' He paused then allowed his gaze, which now held a definite glint of amusement, to meet Rachel's. 'But, yes, Doctor, you're right. Even I have to have a break some time. I've decided to try to grab a few hours on Saturday afternoon. Lucy wants me to take her to the Michaelmas Fair.'

'I thought I might go to that,' said Rachel. 'I must confess I didn't realise they still held them.'

'Perhaps we should go together,' he said softly.

She looked up quickly, suddenly alarmed by something in the tone of his voice, only to be doubly alarmed by the expression in his dark eyes, the amusement replaced now by something else, something altogether more disturbing. 'A date, you mean?' She tried to sound casual but feared she failed miserably, and when he gave a little offhand sort of shrug she hurried on, tripping over her words. 'I'm not sure that's such a good idea, Nick.'

'Really? Why not?' His gaze still held hers and she felt herself begin to melt.

'It just isn't.' She gave a quick little gesture with her hands.

'Give me one good reason.' His voice was low now with a dark, dangerous little edge to it.

'Well...' She was flustered and knew her cheeks would have reddened, hating it and knowing he, too, would have noticed. 'For a start, I'm still in a relationship...'

'Ah, yes, Jeremy.' He inhaled deeply. 'I was forgetting Jeremy.' There was a definite touch of sarcasm in his voice now and Rachel felt herself rise to the bait.

'Besides that,' she went on hotly, 'I don't think it would be a good idea because—'

'Because what?' he interrupted her, raising his dark eyebrows, a gesture that in itself caused a rapid little thrill to shoot down her spine—a thrill she knew she would do well to ignore. But he was waiting...

'Because, well, because we've been there, Nick,' she said at last. 'It didn't work out then and there's no reason to suppose it would be any different now.'

There, she'd said it. She half expected him to argue and was surprised—maybe even a little disappointed—when he merely shrugged.

'OK,' he said, 'no date.'

'Right.' She stood up and bent down to retrieve her case.

'But you can hardly call a Saturday afternoon at the Michaelmas Fair a date, can you?' Nick obviously had no intention of giving up that easily. 'At least, that wouldn't figure as a date in my book,' he went on. 'And, besides, my daughter will be there and you said yourself you were going anyway.' The spark of amusement was back in his eyes now, a spark that was every bit as dangerous and as devastating as his scowl.

Rachel took a deep breath. 'I will no doubt see you there, Nick,' she said firmly. As she turned towards the door, she added, 'Thanks for the lunch.'

'That's OK.' He paused. 'You're not afraid that could be misconstrued as a date?'

'What—lunch in your office?' She raised her eyebrows.

'Some may see it as that.' He shrugged and she had the decided impression he was mocking her.

'It was a working lunch,' she said firmly, 'but if it is misconstrued by others, maybe it's something that shouldn't be repeated.'

'That would be a shame,' Nick replied as he accompanied her back to Reception. 'I found it very pleasant.'

She had, too, but she didn't want to admit as much so instead she merely smiled and with a wave towards Harry, left the building and headed for her car.

It *had* been pleasant, there was no denying that, she told herself as she drove back to the centre, but she had to recognise and acknowledge the warning signs. It would be all too easy to fall into the trap of caring for Nick again, and she could not—must not—let that happen. He had hurt her badly once, she wasn't sure she could survive a second time. Far better to keep him at arm's length where he could do no further damage.

Afternoon surgery was almost over when Rachel received a second email from Tommy Page—at least, she supposed the caller who called himself 'your friend' was indeed Tommy. This time it simply said: *Hello, it's me again.*

Rachel stared at the screen then, on a sudden impulse, which she hoped she wouldn't live to regret, clicked on the 'reply' button, typed, *Who are you?* then hit the 'send' button.

By the end of her surgery a reply had come back. *I think you know who I am,* it said.

It was Tommy—it had to be Tommy. And yet, as she stared at the screen, Rachel had a feeling that somehow this game was a little too subtle for Tommy's capabilities. But if it wasn't Tommy, who was it? Really, deep down, she knew she should tell Nick. There was, after all, a murder investigation going on and she was involved in that even if her part had only been in certifying the death of the victim. But if she told Nick she would presumably have to tell him that she suspected Tommy, and she was very loath to do that. It could pitch Tommy into the centre of the police murder investigation, and if there was one thing she was absolutely certain of it was that there was no way that Tommy was capable of murder. There was no knowing how he would cope with being a suspect, though, and Rachel certainly didn't want to be responsible for bringing him and his mother into an unnecessary spotlight. Far better to remain quiet and hope her mystery 'friend', whether it was Tommy or some unknown admirer, would get tired of the whole thing and give up.

She was about to leave the surgery when Julie buzzed

through to tell her that there was a phone call for her. 'Do you know who it is, Julie?' she asked tentatively, thinking it could possibly be her mystery admirer. Or maybe it was Nick…

'It's Dr James,' Julie replied.

'Oh, put him through,' said Rachel quickly. 'Hello, Daddy.'

'Hello, darling,' her father replied. 'How are you?'

'I'm fine. And you?'

'Yes, pretty good really.'

'And Mummy?' she added tentatively.

'She's having a good spell at the moment,' her father replied, 'so we have to be thankful for small mercies. Last week she upset the gardener. She was terribly rude to him. The poor man said he wasn't going to come any more.'

'Oh, dear,' said Rachel. 'What did you do?'

'Well, I apologised profusely, and begged him to re-consider.'

'And has he?'

'He's still thinking about it. Trouble is, Rachel, people don't like that sort of thing. They don't understand that it's all part of your mother's condition. But that isn't why I'm ringing you. I was wondering if you were think-ing of going to the Michaelmas Fair on Saturday?'

'You're the second person to ask me that today.' Rachel gave a little laugh. 'But, yes, I had thought I might go. Why, are you going?'

'They've asked me to draw the raffle,' her father ex-plained. 'I'm afraid the days are gone when either your mother or myself opened the fair but I think the organ-isers like to make this small gesture by asking me to do the draw.'

'What about Mummy? Will you take her?'

'I was thinking I might,' he replied. 'As I say, she is in the middle of a good spell at the moment but you know how that can change at the drop of a hat and she can be so unpredictable. That's why I was checking to see if you were going, then maybe if necessary you could keep an eye on her while I do my little bit.'

'Of course I can, Daddy.' Rachel's voice softened. 'It's the least I can do. You have this all the time…'

'It isn't all like that, you know.'

'No, I know, but even so.'

'See you on Saturday, then.'

'Yes, see you on Saturday. Bye, Daddy.'

'Goodbye, darling.'

She sat for a moment after she had hung up, reflecting on her parents and their situation since her mother's health had deteriorated with the onset of Alzheimer's disease. The illness had gone through several stages, beginning with a gradual loss of short-term memory. Diana had been angry—with herself and with those around her for her own inadequacies. These days, she had periods where she appeared almost like her old self but which were frequently interspersed with lengthening spells where she hardly knew those around her, and her behaviour was increasingly erratic and unpredictable. Sometimes Rachel wondered how much longer her father would be able to cope and frequently she found herself dreading the future and what it might hold.

The forthcoming Michaelmas Fair looked as if it could be interesting in more ways than one, what with the possibility of unpredictable behaviour from her mother and the fact that for the first time she would be meeting Nick's daughter.

* * *

Saturday morning dawned bright and slightly crisp, with a definite feel of autumn in the air. The large recreation ground behind Westhampstead's leisure centre was the venue for the Michaelmas Fair and for days it had been the scene of intense activity. A funfair, complete with roundabouts, dodgems, sideshows and a big wheel was at one end of the wide, grassy space and white marquees filled with arts and crafts, produce and floral arrangements were at the other. In the centre was an arena, which before the weekend was out would see displays of Morris dancing, dog patrol teams, marching bands, sports, tug-of-war contests and magicians and jugglers. The arena was flanked by refreshment tents, providing everything from beer, cider and barbecued meat to cups of tea and jam scones with clotted cream.

By the time Rachel arrived the fair had already been opened by the Mayor of Westhampstead, a duty that in the past, as her father had recently reminded her, had always been performed either by himself or her mother. There was no sign of either of them and Rachel imagined that her father would leave their arrival until the last possible moment before he was required to perform the draw. She caught sight of Julie and Philip Newton in the crowd, attempting to sell their remaining raffle tickets.

'Hi, Rachel.' Phillip waved to her. 'Can I sell you any more?'

'Oh, go on.' Rachel drew her purse out of her bag and bought several more tickets. 'What time is the draw?' she asked.

'Not till four o'clock,' Philip replied. 'I understand your father is going to perform the honours for us.'

'Yes, that's right.' Rachel nodded. Glancing at her watch, she saw that it was only just after two—plenty of time for her to have a look round before she need be on hand to help with her mother. Slowly she made her way through the steadily growing throng of people towards the display tents. At almost every turn she encountered people she knew, some patients and others faces from the past, some who recognised her, some who didn't. While she was admiring exhibits in the craft tent she caught sight of Georgie across the trestle tables. She waved and indicated to Georgie to make her way to the entrance where a few moments later they met up.

'Phew!' said Georgie, wiping her forehead. 'What a crowd!'

'You're right.' Rachel laughed. 'I think all of Westhampstead must be here.'

'All except my father,' said Georgie with a short laugh. 'He said no way—he didn't intend to be trampled underfoot.'

'Very wise,' said Rachel. 'My parents are coming later.'

'Really?' Georgie sounded surprised.

'My father is doing the draw,' Rachel explained. 'I think he wants me on hand to help with my mother if it should all prove too much for her.' The two of them left the craft tents and began to stroll through the crowd, stopping to buy sticks of shocking-pink candyfloss.

Together they approached the funfair, drawn forward by the sound of music played at full blast, the wail of sirens from the various rides and the screams of youngsters. 'This brings back memories,' said Georgie as a slight breeze caught her candyfloss and plastered it across her face. 'D'you remember how we used to sneak out to the fair and Nick and his gang always seemed to be there? They used to stand around the parapet of the roundabout, in their jeans and leather jackets whistling at all the girls...' She paused, then with a little shriek she said, 'Oh, look, talk of the devil.'

Rachel turned and her heart leapt for he was there, almost as Georgie had described, leaning against the wooden surround of the roundabout. He was once more in leather jacket and jeans, but tailored leather now, not a biker's jacket with studs, and not in the company of his mates, whistling at girls, but with a little girl holding his hand, a little girl who with her dark eyes and hair looked achingly like him.

'Oh,' said Georgie. 'He's seen us. He's coming over.'

'Hello, Georgie.' Nick inclined his head in Georgie's direction. 'Long time, no see.'

'Yes, quite.' Georgie gave a breathless little laugh. 'How are you, Nick?'

'Not so bad.' He was answering Georgie, but his gaze was on Rachel. 'Rachel,' he said with a brief nod.

'Hello, Nick.' Squarely she met his gaze, struggling as she did so to control the racing of her pulse. 'And this...' She looked down at the child. 'This must be Lucy.'

'Yes,' Nick replied, 'this is my daughter. Lucy, this is Dr Beresford.'

'Hello, Dr Beresford,' said Lucy solemnly.

'Hello, Lucy.' Rachel smiled, about to tell the child to call her Rachel then thinking better of it, afraid that Nick wouldn't approve of such familiarity. 'Have you been on any rides yet?' she asked instead.

'We've been on the big roundabout.' Lucy looked over her shoulder towards the large carousel where white horses dipped and rose in time to music from a fairground organ. 'And Daddy said we can go on the dodgems next—didn't you, Daddy?' Eagerly she tugged at his arm and as he looked down at her Rachel felt a pull at her heartstrings at the expression of tenderness in his eyes. This was a new Nick Kowalski, showing a side she had not yet seen—that of devoted father, a far cry from the tough, hard-bitten cop, or the wild boy of the past, or even the exciting lover she had once known.

'Tell you what,' she said. 'How about we *all* go on the dodgems?'

'Oh, yes,' said Lucy, her eyes shining. 'Come on, Daddy, look, they're slowing down.' Tugging at this hand, Lucy pulled him across the grass towards the dodgems, closely followed by Rachel and Georgie.

As they mounted the wooden steps, out of the corner of her eye Rachel caught sight of Tommy Page, together with Eileen, examining the prizes on a nearby hoopla stall. Eileen saw Rachel and waved but Tommy was wearing a Walkman and appeared to be concentrating so intensely that he was unaware of what was happening around him. Rachel felt a stab of relief that he hadn't seen her then immediately felt guilty at feeling that way. Tommy couldn't help the way he was and even if he was her mystery admirer she should simply try to understand and show compassion.

The crowd surged forward at that moment and Rachel, caught up in the scramble for dodgem cars, promptly forgot Tommy. Georgie quickly found a car and beckoned her over, and as she slid into her seat she saw that Nick and Lucy were also seated and Nick was paying the boy who leapt from car to car, taking the tickets.

'Nick's paid for us,' said Georgie as the boy ignored them. 'That was good of him.' As they waited for the cars to move, she said, 'He's as dishy as ever, isn't he?'

'Is he?' said Rachel nonchalantly.

'Oh, come on, Rach,' protested Georgie. 'You know he is—wow, I could go for him myself. I always thought he wasn't my type when we were kids but now, well, he's something else. If you're not interested, just let me know.'

'And what happened to Robbie from Peru?' Rachel raised her eyebrows but she was never to hear Georgie's retort for with a sudden wailing of sirens and screaming of pop music the dodgems leapt into action.

The fun was fast and furious as amidst shrieks of fear and delight they circled round and round and back and forth, dodging and bumping. Several times Rachel caught glimpses of Lucy's excited little face or Nick's profile, his expression tense as he concentrated or relaxed, his head thrown back in a sudden burst of laughter.

It was the happiest Rachel had seen him and at one point she had to remind herself that he was in the midst of a murder investigation. Indeed, it hardly seemed possible that as the residents of Westhampstead relaxed and enjoyed themselves, one of their number, a young girl at that, lay dead in the mortuary. A family had been torn apart for all time and a killer was still at large. She shivered slightly at the thought then reminded herself that life also had to go on. She as a doctor should know that more than most.

It wasn't until after two rides on the dodgems, and as the four of them were making their way through the crowds to the refreshment tents at her invitation, that she caught sight of Terry Payne in the crowd and it came home to her that neither detective was really off duty even for a couple of hours. Even as they mingled with the people of Westhampstead their investigations were ongoing.

By the time Rachel's parents arrived, Rachel, Georgie, Nick and Lucy were seated in the late afternoon sunshine, watching a display of Irish dancing in the arena and enjoying hot dogs and coffee in huge polystyrene cups. As her parents approached, Rachel suddenly felt nervous. In the past there had been no love lost between Nick and her mother especially, but that had been a long time ago and they had all moved on since then. It was doubtful that her mother would even remember Nick. A quick glance reassured Rachel that for the moment at least her mother seemed reasonably calm and happy with no sign of the bouts of anxiety that had plagued her of late.

'Would you like a cup of tea?' Rachel stood up and kissed both parents on the cheek.

'No, thank you, darling,' her father replied. 'We've just had one with the mayor and his wife. I have to do the draw in about ten minutes' time.'

'You remember Nick, don't you?' said Rachel, a slight edge of apprehension in her voice as Nick stood up.

'Yes, of course.' Her father shook hands with Nick while her mother's expression remained perfectly bland. 'I understand you are with the Westhampstead police now?' James said.

'Yes, that's right.' Nick nodded. Any possible moment of awkwardness was hidden as Georgie began to draw more chairs forward in order for the Beresfords to sit down.

They chatted amiably for the next few minutes until Philip and Julie came across and bore James away to the main announcement tent. Carefully, Rachel slid into the vacant chair beside her mother. 'All right, Mummy?' she said. Her mother didn't answer, simply giving a slight nod of her head in response. As Rachel looked up she caught Nick's gaze as he appeared to watch the pair of them. It was impossible to read the expression in his eyes—one of compassion maybe for this woman struck down by such a debilitating disease, or maybe it was one of regret for opportunities missed. She was never to know for at that moment the announcement that the draw was to take place came over the PA system.

The big prizes went first—the foreign holiday, cash prizes, weekend breaks in luxury hotels—then the smaller prizes—DVD players, personal CD systems. Towards the end, one of Rachel's numbers came up.

'Go on,' said Georgie, 'go up. I'll watch your mum,' she whispered when Rachel cast an anxious glance in her mother's direction.

'Well done, Rachel,' said Julie as she presented Rachel with a bottle of brandy.

'Pity it wasn't the holiday,' said Philip with a grin. 'You and I could have had a good time.' He ducked as his wife landed him a good-natured punch on the arm.

James turned to draw another ticket and threw Rachel an anxious glance. 'It's all right, Daddy,' she murmured, reading his thoughts 'Georgie is with Mummy.'

On her return to their table Rachel found that Nick had risen to his feet. 'We should be going,' he said to Rachel.

'Already?' She could barely hide her disappointment and she knew he must have seen it but suddenly she didn't care.

'Afraid so,' he said, then added quietly, so that only she could hear, 'I have to get Lucy home to her mother and then I need to get back to work. I'll be in touch,' he added.

As his gaze once again met hers she suddenly felt as if by meeting there that day and relaxing together something had changed between them. Dragging her gaze away from his, she looked down at Lucy.

'It's been lovely to meet you, Lucy,' she said. 'Maybe I'll see you again one day.'

'I hope so.' Lucy smiled at her and once again Rachel was struck by the resemblance to her father. She could barely remember Marilyn Rooney and what she looked like, but there was no doubting that Lucy was Nick's daughter. The thought gave her a curious pang, a reminder that if things had worked out differently between her and Nick in the past, Lucy could have been hers.

As Nick and Lucy began to move, James arrived back at the table and it was at that moment that Diana suddenly rose rather unsteadily to her feet and, leaning forward, peered into Nick's face.

'I know you!' she exclaimed.

Rachel moved forward, prepared to intervene, but Nick merely smiled and nodded. 'Yes,' he said calmly, 'It's Nick, Nick Kowalski.' He held out his hand but Diana ignored it, instead glaring at Nick then jabbing the air with her finger.

'You,' she said, 'were trouble!'

Lucy looked anxiously up at her father as both Rachel and James moved forward together to placate Diana and lead her away, back to the car.

By the time Rachel returned there was no sign of Nick or Lucy. Only Georgie sat at the table. She rolled her eyes in a gesture of understanding and resignation as Rachel sank thankfully onto a chair.

CHAPTER SIX

'SHE never did like him, did she?' said Georgie after a while during which the two of them simply sat and stared across the arena.

'No,' Rachel agreed with a sigh, 'she didn't, and he knew it as well. Do you know, she was the reason he went into the police force?'

'What?' Georgie stared at her while far out in the arena the Westhampstead Marching Band began playing *Amazing Grace.*

'He overheard her make a comment about him to my father, something on the lines that he was a dead loss and would never amount to anything. He vowed to prove her wrong.'

'And he's done just that,' said Georgie quietly.

'Yes,' Rachel agreed. 'Pity she doesn't really understand.'

'You don't think she does?' Georgie frowned and when Rachel shook her head she said, 'She did recognise him, though, didn't she?'

'Sort of,' Rachel replied, leaning back in her chair and stretching, 'but she probably only knew that it was someone she'd known a long time ago.'

'But she told him he'd been trouble…'

'I know, but I doubt she would have known what that was. That's how she is these days, Georgie. Sometimes she'll remember bits and pieces but she won't be able to set them into context. She may have briefly recognised Nick and she may even have associated his face with some anxiety, but she won't have remembered what that anxiety was.'

'That's terrible,' said Georgie slowly, 'and so hard on your poor dad.'

'Yes, it is,' Rachel agreed, 'but he loves her, he always has, so much so that he'd lay down his own life for her. But I do wonder quite how he'll cope when things get worse, which, of course, they will…' She trailed off and for a while the two of them watched the band as it marched up and down the arena.

'He still cares for you, you know,' said Georgie at last, breaking the silence between them.

'Who, my father?' said Rachel with a weak smile.

'Of course your father.' Georgie gave a dismissive little gesture. 'But I was meaning Nick.'

'Oh?' Rachel shrugged. 'What makes you think that?' She spoke casually but she was instantly on guard, wondering what her friend was about to say.

'Several things really,' Georgie replied, 'but mostly the way he looks at you, especially when he thinks you aren't looking. And he couldn't wait for you to meet his daughter.'

'You think so?'

'I know so. I could tell, just as I could tell that it is important to him that you two should like each other and get along.'

'Well, I don't know about that…' said Rachel slowly, but deep inside she felt a small warm throb of happiness at Georgie's words. 'She's a lovely little girl, isn't she?'

'Yes, she is,' Georgie agreed, 'and very like her father.' She paused. 'Did you know her mother has a new partner?'

'No, I didn't.' Rachel looked up quickly. 'How do you know that?'

'A friend of a friend,' said Georgie vaguely. 'Apparently it's someone Marilyn was at school with who's recently moved back into the area.'

'Isn't it strange how people move away from their home town and then very often gravitate back?' Rachel mused. 'Take us, for example, and Nick, and this guy you've just mentioned who's with Marilyn Rooney.'

'Kowalski,' said Georgie.

'Sorry?' Rachel frowned.

'You said Marilyn Rooney. Didn't you mean Marilyn Kowalski?'

'Oh, yes, I suppose I did.' It sounded strange. Marilyn Kowalski. She didn't like it. With a frown she stood up. 'I'll have to be going,' she said, looking down at Georgie who squinted up at her, shielding her eyes from the last rays of the afternoon sun.

'Oh, do you have to go?' Georgie sounded disappointed.

'Yes, I have a house call I want to make before I go home.'

'OK.' Georgie stood up, 'I guess I may as well go home as well.'

Together they made their way back through the dwindling crowd to the field where their cars were parked.

The house call Rachel wanted to make was to the elderly man she had previously visited who was in the final stages of terminal cancer. His family were all with him and he was in the day-to-day care of the community nurses, having recently been discharged from the local hospital. Rachel spoke with the community nurse who was just leaving the house as she arrived, then checked and adjusted the patient's medication before giving a few words of comfort and encouragement to the man's wife.

After leaving the house she called at the medical centre, which was closed for the weekend, to leave the cancer patient's records in case another doctor required them before the surgery was open again. She was about to leave when a sudden impulse sent her up the stairs to her consulting room to log on to her computer and check her emails. As she had half expected, there was a message from 'your friend'. She clicked on the message and opened it. It read: *You looked lovely today. Jeans suit you.*

She stared at the screen. It *had* to be Tommy. He had been there earlier that day at the fair. She hadn't thought he'd seen her but he must have done, maybe not when she'd seen him, but later, possibly when she'd been sitting outside the refreshment tent with Georgie, Nick and Lucy, or perhaps even when her parents had been there. She would have to have a word with Tommy, tell him to stop all this, that this sort of behaviour was not acceptable. But would he understand that? Maybe she should have a word with Eileen. Perhaps she could have some influence over her son and what he did.

Troubled by what she had discovered, Rachel left the building, carefully resetting the alarm system and locking the double front doors behind her.

On her return to Cathedral Close she spent a couple of hours catching up on some paperwork then, before preparing a meal for herself, she phoned her father.

'Hello, darling.' He sounded really pleased at hearing her voice.

'I was just wondering how Mummy was after you got home.'

'She was very tired,' he replied. 'I think all the people and events over-stimulated her. She's sleeping now.'

'That's good,' Rachel said. 'And what about you—how are you?'

'Oh, I'm all right,' her father replied, but there was a weariness in his voice that made Rachel's heart ache. 'It's your mother who's my main concern.' He paused then went on, 'I hope young Kowalski wasn't offended by her.'

'I wouldn't have thought so,' Rachel replied, 'not for one moment.'

'He always knew your mother didn't like him, didn't he?'

'Yes, Daddy.' She gave a little sigh. 'I guess he did. But you didn't like him either, did you?'

'I didn't think he was right for you,' her father replied carefully, 'at least, not at that time. But I can honestly say I didn't dislike him. And I do have to say he's done very well now—what rank is he in the police force?'

'Detective Chief Inspector.'

'Yes, I thought so. I really am amazed at what he's achieved.'

'So, if you and Mummy had known then what you know now, would he have been deemed suitable for your only daughter?'

'Oh, Rachel, how can I answer that?' He paused again. 'But you are happy now, aren't you, darling?'

'How do you mean—happy?'

'Well, with Jeremy?'

'Oh, that sort of happy.' She gave a short laugh. 'Well, now, let's see…'

'You have to think about it?' Her father sounded mildly surprised.

'Let's just say it's going through one of those rough patches,' said Rachel. 'Maybe it will survive, maybe it won't. I really don't know, but I dare say this year apart will sort things out one way or the other.'

'I'm sorry, Rachel, I had no idea.'

'You couldn't have known. I hadn't said anything.'

'Young Kowalski's marriage didn't work out either, did it?'

'No, Daddy, it didn't.' She gave another laugh. 'Maybe Nick and I might have been right for each other all those years ago—who knows?'

'Do you blame your mother and me for that?'

'What? No, of course not,' she went on rapidly, not waiting for a reply. 'Nick dumped me soon after I got to medical school—found someone else. Mummy told me that. No, it wasn't your fault. I guess he simply couldn't cope with me being away, that's all.'

'Were you very upset at the time?' He sounded worried.

'Suicidal,' she said cheerfully.

'Rachel…?' There was real anxiety in his voice now.

'Only joking,' she said. 'I wasn't quite that bad, but I was pretty heartbroken. At that age I guess something like that seems like the end of the world.'

'You don't think now there's a possibility—?'

'Shouldn't think so,' she interrupted him quickly, not wanting him to even put it into words. 'No. It's a mistake to go back. Things can never be the same again.'

'No, maybe not,' he agreed. 'But I would like to see you happy again, Rachel.'

'Settled down with two point four children, you mean?'

'Something like that, I suppose, yes.'

'Well, maybe one day, Daddy. Who knows? Anyway, I'd better go now and get myself something to eat.'

'Are you on call tonight?'

'Not for the practice,' she replied, 'but I am on call for the police.'

'Are they any closer to catching that young girl's murderer?'

'I don't know. I believe they had one or two leads to follow up.'

'I delivered her, you know,' he said slowly, 'little Kaylee Munns.'

'Oh, Daddy, did you?' She felt a sudden stab of compassion.

'Yes, I did. Pretty little baby she was.'

'I'm so sorry—you must have been upset to hear about her death.'

'Yes, I was, actually,' he admitted. 'I tried to tell your mother about it, but she didn't know what I was talking about. Anyway, I'd better let you go now—but do take care, won't you, Rachel?'

'Yes, Daddy, of course I will. And…I'll try to come over for lunch in a day or so.'

'That would be lovely—your mother will like that. Goodnight, darling.'

'Night, Daddy.'

It was much later that same evening, after she'd eaten her solitary supper, showered and was preparing for bed, that her phone rang. Offering up a silent prayer that it wouldn't be her mystery caller, she picked up the phone.

'Rachel.'

'Nick?' Her fingers tightened involuntarily around the receiver.

'Can you come to the station?'

'What's the problem?'

'There's been an incident—a young woman has been attacked but managed to escape her attacker. We need you to examine her.'

'I'm on my way.'

'No! Rachel, listen, we'll send a car for you.'

'There's no need,' she protested.

'There's every need. I can't come myself but a squad car will pick you up.'

'OK. If you insist.'

'I do insist.' The line went dead and as Rachel replaced the receiver she felt that by now familiar surge of adrenalin at the thought of working with Nick again.

The car arrived ten minutes later, giving Rachel just time enough to dress in trousers and a dark roll-necked sweater, to tie back her hair, which was still damp from the shower, and to grab her case, her jacket and her keys. There was bright moonlight that night and the sky was clear and starry with a chill in the air.

As Rachel left the house and a young police officer opened the rear passenger door of the patrol vehicle for her, she noticed a second car in the close. It was parked a few houses down, close to the cathedral, and from the light of the streetlamps she noticed that someone was sitting in the darkness in the passenger seat. She imagined it was simply someone waiting as the driver of the car visited another of the residents of the close.

'Good evening, ma'am.' The officer stood aside to allow her to enter the vehicle.

'Good evening.' Rachel ducked her head, climbed into the car and fastened her seat-belt. The vehicle drew away, gathering speed as it nosed out of the close and onto the wider, deserted roads around the cathedral.

On arrival at police headquarters Rachel was met by Nick and Terry, both of whom appeared grim-faced and unsmiling.

'Thanks for coming, Rachel,' said Nick briefly. 'Come

to my office and I'll bring you up to date on what's happening.'

She followed Nick down the corridor to his by now familiar office, where he indicated for her to take a seat. Nick himself sat behind his desk while Terry leaned against the closed door.

'Officers were called to a house in Maybury Street this evening.' Nick launched straight into the details. 'There, they found a young woman, Rowena Woodhouse, aged twenty-six, in a highly distressed state. She was in the company of her parents and her boyfriend. It appeared that she had attended a farewell celebration for one of her colleagues at the local library where she is a librarian. They had been to an Italian restaurant in town but Rowena had felt unwell and had left before the others— she'd been unable to call a cab so she began to walk home.' Nick paused then, taking a deep breath, continued, 'Someone jumped out on her in an alleyway between the restaurant and the canal and attacked her— she claims she was raped. Her screams attracted the attention of some passers-by who came to her rescue, causing her attacker to run off. These people took her home where her parents called us. We'd like you to examine her, please, Rachel. Usual swabs so that forensics can test for DNA and anything else that she may be able to tell you.'

'She's pretty traumatised at the moment,' said Terry, 'but she may well feel able to talk to you.'

'You mentioned a boyfriend,' said Rachel. 'Where was he in all this?'

'Apparently he was at home, watching television,' Nick replied. 'Rowena's father phoned him after she had been brought home and he went to their house immediately. The officers who attended said he was in a distraught state. He came to the station with Rowena and his statement is being taken at the moment.'

'Right.' Rachel stood up. 'I'd best get on with it, then.'

'I'll take you along to the medical room,' said Nick, as Terry opened the door.

Rowena was sitting huddled in a chair, shaking uncontrollably, a tartan blanket around her shoulders, her thin hands encircling a mug of tea. She didn't even look up as Rachel and the two detectives came into the room and briefly acknowledged the WPC on duty.

'Rowena.' Nick crouched in front of the woman who jumped violently then cringed away from him. 'This is Dr Beresford. She has come to talk to you and to examine you.' He straightened up and nodded at Rachel. 'We'll leave you to it,' he murmured. Turning, he beckoned to Terry, who had been hovering near the door, and the two of them left the room, shutting the door behind them, leaving Rachel with the WPC and Rowena.

'Rowena.' It was Rachel's turn to crouch in front of the girl, who didn't react in quite the same way as she had to Nick. 'I know this is very hard for you after what you have been through tonight but I do need to get a clearer picture as to what exactly happened to you.'

The woman's hands tightened around the mug and as she glanced up briefly Rachel noticed the tears that ran silently down her cheeks. 'I understand,' she said, drawing up a chair and sitting in front of Rowena, 'that you went out for a meal with some friends from work, is that right? Rowena?' she prompted when the woman remained silent.

'Yes,' Rowena replied at last, her voice barely more than a whisper.

'Can you tell me what happened?'

Another silence then with a huge shuddering sigh she began to talk, her voice still low. 'We went to Guiseppe's,' she said, 'the Italian restaurant in Prince's Street. Towards the end of the meal...I...I didn't feel too well... I thought I was starting a migraine.'

'So what did you do?'

'I decided to go home...without waiting for the others...'

'Did you say anything to them?'

'I told Gill—she's a librarian, same as me—that I was going. She wanted to come with me...but I said no, that she should stay...that...that I would be all right... Oh!' She choked at the implication of what she had just said.

'Did you try to ring for a taxi?'

'Yes...from my mobile...in the ladies loo...but I couldn't get one. I tried three—two I couldn't get through to and the third wouldn't have been available for three quarters of an hour... So I decided to walk. It isn't really that far from the restaurant to my home, not if you go by the canal...'

'I understand you live with your parents, Rowena?' said Rachel, leaning forward as Rowena's hands began shaking so hard that the tea in the mug started slopping over the sides. Gently she extricated the mug and set it down on the floor.

'Yes.' Rowena nodded. 'I could have phoned my father to come and get me, I know, or even my boyfriend, Stephen, but I thought the walk might do me good...'

'How long have you been seeing your boyfriend, Rowena?'

'Three months. We met at the Baptist church that we both attend.'

'So you left the restaurant alone. Can you tell me what happened next?'

'I walked down the road and then… There's this alleyway that leads down to the canal… I was only halfway down the alley when…' She choked again and shook her head, dashing tears away with her hand.

'Here.' Rachel passed her a couple of tissues from a box on the couch beside them. 'Take your time, Rowena, and try to tell me what happened.'

Rowena drew a long, deep breath, 'I heard someone…behind me…footsteps… I started to hurry…but they went faster, too. I was almost running when someone caught hold of me from behind. I…lost my balance and we both crashed to the ground. It—the fall must have stunned me because the next thing I knew…this… this person was on top of me. I tried to scream but he stuffed something in my mouth…some horrible oily rag. I thought I was going to suffocate. He was tearing at my clothes… I struggled and struggled but I couldn't…' She began to weep again profusely.

'Did he rape you, Rowena?' asked Rachel gently, holding the girl's hands tightly.

'Yes…'

Rachel remained silent for a long moment. The only noise in the room was the ticking of a clock over the door and the muffled sound of Rowena's sobs. 'And what happened afterwards?' asked Rachel at last.

'I…I thought he was going to kill me,' whispered Rowena. 'He had his hands around my throat and was squeezing. There was a noise at the end of the alleyway—it distracted him… I managed to get the rag out of my mouth and screamed. I screamed as loud as I could…'

'And what happened?'

'There were people at the end of the alley—they must have heard me. He…he…must have panicked. He punched me.' She lifted her hand to a reddened area at the side of her face, 'then he ran off. The people came and found me and took me home… My father called the police…'

'Did you get a look at him—would you be able to give the police a description?' asked Rachel after a moment.

'No,' Rowena replied slowly. 'He had something over his head, something dark—a balaclava, I think.'

'Can you remember anything at all about him?'

'He smelt of cigarettes—tobacco.'

'Well done, Rowena,' said Rachel. 'I will have to examine you,' she added. 'You do understand that?'

'Don't you believe me?' asked Rowena, looking up at her, her eyes filled with dull pain.

'Of course I do,' Rachel replied. 'But it isn't a question of whether or not I believe you. When this man is caught we need to have proof of what he did to you. Now, I have to ask you—you haven't bathed or showered since the attack, have you?'

Rowena shuddered violently again. 'No,' she said. 'I wanted to—I really did, I feel so dirty, but—'

'You can, just as soon as I've carried out my examination and taken samples for DNA testing,' Rachel said. 'If you wouldn't mind climbing up onto the couch, we will get this over just as quickly as possible.'

When Rachel had completed her examination and taken the necessary DNA samples, she left Rowena in the capable hands of the WPC and returned to Nick's office. He was on his own, with no sign of Terry either in the office or in the larger control room where night staff presumably were still dealing with Kaylee Munns's murder.

'All finished?' asked Nick as she came into the room, closing the door behind her.

'Yes,' Rachel replied. 'I've examined her and taken samples that will, of course, go to the lab for testing. I'll write up a report and let you have it as soon as possible. She has refused the morning-after Pill on religious grounds but she has agreed to an HIV test.'

'Any preliminary thoughts?' Nick's eyes narrowed.

Rachel perched on the edge of his desk. 'I would say she certainly was raped—there were definite signs of a fierce struggle. I would also go so far as to say that it was only through the intervention of the passers-by that she escaped with her life.'

'She told you he tried to kill her?'

'Yes.' Rachel nodded. 'She said he had his hands around her throat and was squeezing. Apparently he'd previously pushed some sort of rag into her mouth but she managed to pull it out and scream for help. Just before the people came to her rescue she said he punched her on the side of her face.'

'Is there evidence of that?' asked Nick.

'Oh, yes,' Rachel replied. 'A huge bruise is already forming.'

'You spoke of other signs of a struggle—can you be more specific?'

'Well, several fingernails were broken—she'd scratched him and I was able to take samples from under the nails that were still intact. She had several areas of bruising on her body and there were definite marks around her neck, which would confirm her story of him having tried to strangle her. It will all be in my report, Nick.'

'OK, thanks.' With a sigh he leaned back in his chair and linked his hands behind his head. 'No other impressions?' he asked.

'What do you mean?'

'Well, did she talk about her family, her boyfriend—anything like that?'

'She did.' Rachel frowned. 'But hasn't she given a statement to your boys?'

'She wasn't saying too much when she came in—she was pretty traumatised. In these cases the victim will very often open up to a doctor where they won't to any of us.'

'She only really mentioned her parents in passing, in that she didn't call them when she couldn't get a cab because she decided the walk might help her headache—likewise her boyfriend.'

'Did she say anything else about him?'

'Only that they have only been going out for about three months and that they met at their local church. You're not thinking he did this, are you?' Her eyes narrowed as she looked down at him.

'Rachel, I'm keeping an open mind at the moment. If there's one thing I've learnt over the years it's that everyone in any case is a potential suspect.'

'Yes, quite,' she agreed. 'Well, just as long as you get the right man. Rape is a nasty business, Nick. That young woman will be severely traumatised for years, and there's a very good chance she won't ever get over it.'

'I know.' He inhaled deeply then, his gaze meeting hers, he added, 'I do know, but my immediate concern has to be that I now not only have an unsolved murder on my hands but also rape and an attempted murder. Two worryingly similar crimes.'

'Big stuff for Westhampstead,' said Rachel softly.

'You can say that again.' Lowering his arms, Nick pushed back his chair and stood up. 'Come on,' he said. 'I'll take you home.'

'You don't have to,' she replied lightly, at the same time desperately hoping he would. 'I'm sure that charming PC who brought me here will do the honours again.'

'No need,' he said. 'I'm going home myself—contrary to popular belief, we CID cops do occasionally need to sleep.'

Together they walked to Reception and were just in time to see Rowena Woodhouse leaving the building in the company of a middle-aged couple and a rather intense-looking young man with a shaven head and wire-rimmed glasses.

Five minutes later Rachel slipped into the passenger seat of Nick's car and leaned back against the headrest. Suddenly she felt overwhelmingly tired and fought against closing her eyes, fearful that if she did so she would be asleep in seconds. Instead, as they drove through the deserted streets of Westhampstead she cast Nick a sidelong glance. 'She's lovely, Nick,' she said.

'I'm sorry?' He threw her a startled glance.

'Lucy,' she said. 'Your daughter—she's lovely.'

'Oh,' he said. 'I thought you were talking about Rowena—sorry. Ah, yes, Lucy—she is lovely, isn't she?'

'Quite obviously your pride and joy.'

'Absolutely.' His voice softened. 'Do you know, Rachel, I never knew it was possible to feel like that about a child. I just want to protect her from all the things that might harm her.'

At his words Rachel had to fight a swift stab of some emotion that was difficult to define. It might have been jealousy, or perhaps envy, but of Marilyn rather than

Lucy, because it should have been her, Rachel, who knew what it was to have a child with Nick.

'She liked you, you know,' he went on, oblivious to her thoughts. 'She said afterwards what a nice lady you were. And very pretty, too—that's what she said. I, of course, could only agree with her.'

Rachel was glad of the darkness to cover her confusion. 'I...I hope I shall see her again,' she said.

'I'm sure that can be arranged.' Nick paused. 'I thought your mother was looking rather frail,' he went on after a moment.

'She is,' Rachel agreed, 'you mustn't mind her, you know, and what she says...'

'I never did,' he said with a short laugh.

'I know.' Briefly she joined in his laughter, relieved that the rather sombre mood between them, which had been determined no doubt by the nature of the business they had been involved with, had now lifted a little. 'But I spoke to my father this evening and he seemed rather concerned that you may have taken offence at what she said.'

'It would take more than that.' Nick shrugged. 'Thick-skinned lot us cops, you know—we have to be,' he added dryly.

'Yes, I can imagine...' She trailed off and looked out of the window. The cathedral loomed above them on one side, a huge dark shadow obscuring the moon, and then Nick drew into the close, brought the car to a halt in front of St Edmund's and switched off the engine.

'I know,' she said in the darkness, 'that this is a ridiculous time of night to be suggesting this, and you're probably desperate to get home and get some sleep, but I'm going to make a pot of tea—would you like to join me?'

'I would hate to go down in history as the only cop known to refuse a cup of tea so, yes, please, Rachel,' he said with a sudden, deep and utterly infectious chuckle. 'I'd be delighted to join you.'

CHAPTER SEVEN

'THIS is very nice,' Nick said as he followed Rachel through the hall and into the kitchen.

'Yes,' she agreed with a short laugh. 'Pity it isn't mine.'

'Who does it belong to again?' asked Nick as he prowled around, inspecting furniture and fittings.

'Friends of my parents. They're abroad,' Rachel explained. 'I'd never be able to afford to buy anything like this.'

'Me neither,' Nick agreed, 'but that doesn't mean I wouldn't like to.'

'Yes, I'm afraid I'll get so used to it that I won't want to give it up when the owners return.' She paused and looked at Nick. 'Tell me,' she said, suddenly realising that she didn't know, 'where is home for you these days?'

'Well, nothing as grand as this for a start. I have a two-bedroomed apartment in that new complex on the other side of the park, down near the canal.'

'I've seen those,' Rachel said as she filled the kettle. 'They look rather nice.'

'They're adequate.' Nick shrugged. 'Bit basic, but they suit my purpose for the time being.'

'That being?'

'To be close to work and to have somewhere for Lucy to come and visit.'

'Ah, yes, of course.' Opening the fridge, she took out a plastic milk container.

'She was right, you know,' said Nick, leaning on the worktop and watching her as she poured milk into two mugs then returned the container to the fridge.

'About what?' Briefly she allowed her gaze to meet his, then at what she saw she looked quickly away again.

'About you being pretty,' he said. 'You always were,' he went on before she could utter any sort of protest. 'But now, well...' He paused. 'You've changed, you know, Rachel,' he said at last.

'Oh, dear,' she said, 'that sounds ominous. Although I suppose it's inevitable really after all this time that one would look older...'

'I wasn't talking about looking older,' he said quietly.

'Well, I'm sorry I'm no longer pretty,' she said with a short laugh as the water boiled and she leaned over to fill the teapot.

'You're beautiful,' he said softly, and suddenly she realised he was right behind her, so close that if she moved as much as an inch they would be touching. She froze, allowing herself only the simple movement of re-placing the teapot lid. 'Your hair,' he went on. 'It's lovely. You used to wear it shorter but I like it long like that.' She sensed rather than saw him reach out his hand, then was aware that he was touching her hair. This wasn't happening, she told herself. She couldn't let this happen. It had taken her months, no, years to get over him the last time, if she ever had. She simply couldn't let it happen again. She moved away from him on the pretext of taking the sugar bowl from the cupboard above the worktops. Stretching up, she opened the cupboard doors and it was then that she felt his arms go round her.

'Rachel...' His voice sounded more like a groan as he spoke her name and even as she stiffened in defence, her whole body as taut now as that of an animal that has sensed danger and been caught in a trap, he lowered his head and began kissing the vulnerable hollow between her neck and shoulder. Thoughts raced unbidden through her mind. It would be so easy to give in to this moment, to allow Nick back into her life, to let him hold her, kiss her, just as he had before. But it wouldn't end there, Rachel knew that. It would simply be one short step to her bedroom where he would undress her and make love to her. A delicious shudder spread through her veins at the thought—it would be just like it had been between them all those years ago… But as his arms tightened around her and he grew more insistent, from somewhere she drew up the strength of mind to pull away from him in spite of the yearning ache of desire that was unfolding deep inside. The pain would soon outweigh the pleasure, intense and satisfying as she knew that would be.

'No, Nick.' Adeptly she extricated herself from his arms, put the sugar bowl on the tray with the teapot and mugs then, picking up the tray, moved past him on her way to the sitting room, ignoring both the deep sigh that came from his lips and the expression of resignation on his face.

'OK,' he said as he followed her, 'but I'm not sure why.'

'You know why,' she replied briskly, setting the tray down on a low table and busying herself with drawing the thick velvet curtains. 'We've been there, Nick, and it didn't work.'

'You don't think it might be different now with the benefit of hindsight and experience?'

'No, Nick, I don't,' she replied firmly, trying to ignore the clamouring of her heart, which was urging her to let nature take its course with this devastatingly attractive man. And maybe she should at that, she thought as she sat down opposite him and watched as he sat down on the sofa, one arm along the back, his long legs thrust out in front of him. After all, what would it matter if she had a one-night stand with an old lover? Who would know? Who would care?

'Is it Jeremy?' he said suddenly.

She stared at him. She'd completely forgotten about Jeremy. 'Is what Jeremy?'

'The reason you won't come to bed with me?' he said bluntly.

'Yes,' she lied, 'sort of.'

'What do you mean, *sort of*?' His lips twitched.

'Well, I *am* in a relationship with Jeremy,' she protested.

'Such as it is,' he said.

She had the distinct impression he was mocking her so she ignored his last remark, instead leaning forward and pouring out the tea. Her decision not to go to bed with Nick had been because of the way she would suffer afterwards when he would simply get on with his life as if nothing had happened. It had nothing whatsoever to do with Jeremy but she didn't want Nick to know that. And the more she thought about that, she realised that because she felt that way, her whole relationship with Jeremy would have to come under even greater scrutiny than it already had.

'Can we talk about something else?' she said, as she passed a mug of tea to Nick.

'If you like.' He gave a lazy smile. 'What would you like to talk about?'

'The case tonight, Rowena…?'

'You want to talk shop.' He sounded disappointed.

'It was just a thought I had, really.'

'Go on,' he said, taking a mouthful of his tea and setting the mug down. 'We need all the help we can get at the moment.'

'Do you think the cases are linked?' she asked slowly. 'Kaylee Munns's murder and now this?'

'There's a possibility, certainly,' he replied, deadly serious now. 'Two young women, both attacked late at night, both the victims of sexual assault, one murdered and the other an attempted murder, both strangulation...but were you thinking of something more specific?'

'Not really. Only that...' She hesitated.

'Go on,' he prompted.

'The canal was mentioned in both cases,' she said at last, and then suddenly aware of his growing interest she went on, 'Kaylee Munns was found by the canal and Rowena planned to walk down the alleyway and go home the shorter route, again by the canal.'

'It could be significant,' he said. 'On the other hand, it could be a copycat attack—that does happen in cases like this.'

'But if it was the same man...?'

'We could have a serial killer on our hands,' he said bluntly.

'So he could strike again?' Rachel gave a shiver.

'If he's a serial killer he will most certainly kill again,' Nick replied. 'Our job is to catch him before he does. Which means I'd better get home and get a few hours' sleep before joining the fray again.' He paused and threw her a sidelong glance. 'That is, if you aren't going to allow me to stay here, in which case I would gladly forego the sleep.'

'Nick...I...'

'It's all right.' He grinned. 'Only joking.'

'I'm sorry, Nick.' She shook her head. 'But I really don't think it would work.'

'OK.' He held up his hands in a gesture of surrender. 'I dare say you're right. They say you shouldn't go back, don't they? That you shouldn't try to reconstruct the past, that it's never the same second time around. I just thought it might be good, finding out. But if you don't think it's a good idea then it's probably best to leave things the way they are.' He drained his mug then, putting his open palms on his thighs as if in preparation to standing up, he threw her a wicked glance, 'Pity, though, because it was good between us, wasn't it?' When she remained silent, he said, 'No? Maybe you don't remember it that way.'

He stood up and looked down at her and Rachel felt her insides churn. With a sigh she also stood up. 'Of course it was good, Nick,' she said softly. It was no good denying it—his memories would be the same as hers. 'It was very good, you know it as well as I do, but I still don't think that alone is a reason for a repeat performance. There has to be more to a relationship than good sex.'

'That may or may not be true.' He shrugged. 'But I say that it's a very good place to start.' Reaching out his hand, he very gently stroked the side of her cheek with the backs of his fingers. It was almost her undoing, almost had her begging him to stay, so it was probably just as well that after that he moved towards the door.

She followed him into the hall and when he paused at the front door she leaned past him and opened it. Once again they were close, so close that she caught the male tang of him—a heady mixture of soap, aftershave, leather and something else, something indefinable, the very essence of the man—as for a moment she felt the warmth of his breath on her cheek. Once again she was forced to hold herself firmly in check to restrain her desire when really she would have liked nothing better than to wind her arms around his neck, sink her fingers into his hair and press her body against his.

'Don't forget the chain,' he said, touching the brass door chain with his fingers.

'I won't,' she replied, realising that because of the nature of her thoughts she sounded a little breathless and hoping he wouldn't notice.

'Goodnight, Rachel,' he said softly. 'Thanks for the tea.'

'Goodnight, Nick.' She watched as he walked out to his car then, as he unlocked it with the remote control and opened the door, she glanced along the road towards the cathedral. The car that had been there before was once again parked by the kerb a couple of houses away—at least, she thought it was the same car. It certainly looked the same, although it was hard to tell in the dark. This time, however, it wasn't parked directly under the streetlamp so it wasn't possible to tell whether or not anyone was sitting inside as there had been before. As Nick started his engine she looked back at his car and was just in time to see him raise one hand in farewell. Quickly she did the same then, waiting only long enough to see the red tail lights of his car as it drew away, she closed the front door, locked it and secured the chain.

Wandering back into the sitting room, she asked herself if she wasn't being a fool. Really and truly, if she was completely honest with herself, she had wanted Nick to stay, so if that was the case why had she acted like some silly immature teenager and sent him away? He must have thought that she hadn't grown up at all in the years since they'd last seen each other. He'd thought it was simply her relationship with Jeremy that prevented her from renewing any sort of relationship with him, but deep down Rachel knew it was more than that—deep down she knew that she couldn't bear to go through a second rejection from Nick.

Picking up the tray, she carried it out to the kitchen and set it down on the worktop. Maybe it wouldn't be like that this time, maybe Nick had matured and would want a more committed relationship. But on the other hand, and given his track record, it was more than likely that he hadn't. With a sigh she stacked the mugs into the dishwasher then switched out the kitchen light before going up the stairs to bed.

Sleep didn't come easily that night for as she tossed and turned for at least a couple of hours, she couldn't help but imagine what it would have been like if she'd allowed Nick to stay.

'Now that I have all the test results I'm going to arrange for you to see a cardiologist.' It was the following Monday morning and Georgie had come into the centre, together with Harvey, at Rachel's request in order to discuss the tests that had recently been carried out.

'Is it anything serious?' For once Harvey Reynolds's blue eyes were clouded.

'I hope not,' Rachel replied, 'but I want to be certain. I'll refer you to Edward Drummond.'

'I know Ted Drummond,' Harvey said thoughtfully. 'We play golf together.'

'Well, there you are,' said Rachel with a smile, rising to her feet as Georgie and her father did likewise. 'It shouldn't take long for the appointment to come through. In the meantime, I want you to watch your diet—keep to the low-fat one we talked about and keep up your exercise.'

'I'll make sure of that,' said Georgie.

As Rachel opened the door the intercom buzzed on her desk. 'Will you excuse me?' she said, and with a quick glance at Georgie she added, 'I'll be in touch.'

'Bye, Rachel,' said Georgie, 'and thanks for everything.'

'Rachel,' said Danielle through the intercom, 'there's been a delivery down here for you.'

'Really? I'll come down,' Rachel replied. 'Do I have any more patients?'

'No, Mr Reynolds was the last.'

By the time Rachel reached Reception Georgie and her father had left. 'So what is it?' she asked, leaning over the desk.

'These,' Danielle replied. 'Aren't they gorgeous?' From under the desk she brought out a bunch of yellow rosebuds wrapped in tissue paper.

'Oh.' Rachel stared at them for a moment. Yellow roses were her favourite flowers.

'There's a card,' said Danielle.

There was indeed a tiny envelope nestled deep inside the flowers and when Rachel drew it out she saw it had her name, Dr Beresford, written on it. She withdrew the card inside, which simply said, 'For Rachel with love'.

'We didn't see who delivered them, did we, Julie?' Danielle turned to her colleague.

'No,' Julie replied. 'They were just left on the desk, none of us saw who by, but it doesn't look like they were delivered by a florist, does it? If they had they would have been done up in yards of Cellophane with pink ribbons. Probably from a grateful patient.'

'Or a secret admirer,' said Danielle with a wistful sigh.

Rachel pulled a face then, taking the flowers, went slowly back up the stairs to her consulting room. There was only one person who knew that yellow roses were her favourite flowers, the same person who had bought her yellow roses years ago when she'd heard she'd got into medical school. Even Jeremy didn't know she liked yellow roses. Somehow she'd never been able to tell him, afraid that he, too, would buy them for her, knowing that if he did, somehow it wouldn't be the same.

She couldn't quite believe that he had remembered after all these years. Sitting at her desk, she lifted the receiver and dialled a number. A woman's voice at the other end told her she was through to Westhampstead Police Headquarters. 'Could I speak to DCI Kowalski, please?' she said.

'May I ask who's calling?' asked the woman.

'Dr Beresford,' she replied. 'Rachel Beresford.'

'I'll put you through.'

'Rachel?' Nick sounded surprised—hadn't he thought she'd phone to thank him? He also, she thought, sounded pleased.

'Nick,' she said, and found she was struggling to keep her voice casual. 'I just wanted to thank you. It was a lovely thought. I'm amazed you remembered.'

There was a long silence from the other end of the phone then she heard Nick's voice again, slightly mystified this time. 'Rachel, I'm sorry but you have the advantage over me. Just what is it that I'm supposed to have remembered?'

'That yellow roses are my favourite flowers?' Even as she said it she had the feeling that somehow something was wrong here.

'You've received some yellow roses?' asked Nick.

'Yes, they were left at the reception desk this morning.' She swallowed, beginning to feel decidedly uncomfortable.

'Well, I'm sorry I can't lay claim to having left them…'

'Oh, it's all right,' she said quickly. 'I'm sorry, I thought they were from you. I was mistaken, they must be from…someone else…' she ended lamely.

'Well, I know I haven't missed your birthday,' said Nick. 'That isn't until next month—the twenty-fourth, isn't it?'

'Heavens,' said Rachel in amazement. 'Fancy you remembering that.'

'I bet you don't remember when mine is.'

'I do, actually.'

'Go on, then, when is it?'

'The ninth of May.'

'I'm impressed,' he said softly.

'Nick…I have to go,' she said, 'I have patients to see.'

'OK. Bye, then. Oh, Rachel?'

'Yes?'

'I still wish I'd thought of sending you yellow roses,' he said.

After she'd hung up she sat for a long while thinking about the flowers and who had sent them. If it hadn't been for the fact that Nick had sent her those yellow roses in the past she would never have suspected that it might have been him. Now that he had been eliminated it seemed fairly probable that they could be from her mystery admirer. It would have been a relatively easy task for Tommy to have bought the roses, written on the card then left them on the main reception desk when no one was looking. The fact that he had hit on yellow roses had been no more than a strange coincidence. But Rachel knew that she had to do something to put a stop to these events, which now were becoming disturbing.

Swiftly coming to a decision, she leaned across to her computer and brought up the personal details of Eileen Page, including her phone number.

Eileen answered on the third ring. 'Eileen, it's Dr Beresford,' said Rachel.

'Hello, Doctor.' Eileen sounded almost as surprised as Nick had done. 'Is there anything wrong?'

'No, Eileen,' Rachel hastened to reassure her, mindful of how anxious people became if contacted unexpectedly by their GP. 'There's nothing wrong, but I was wondering if I could have a chat with you about Tommy.'

'Well, yes, of course,' Eileen replied. 'But when, and do you want Tommy there as well?'

'No, I want to see you on your own. When does Tommy go to the day centre?'

'Well, he's there today.'

'So could I call in to see you…' Rachel glanced at her watch '…say, about twelve o'clock?'

'Yes, all right, Dr Beresford,' Eileen replied.

'I'll see you then,' she said.

Rachel wasn't convinced she was handling this in the right way but she knew she had to do something. Deep down she knew that really she should be telling Nick about the unwanted attention she was receiving, especially with what had been happening recently in Westhampstead, but her gut instinct was still that it was Tommy who had developed a crush on her and the last thing she wanted was for him to come under any sort of police investigation. Hopefully a word with his mother might be all it would need to put a stop to his activities.

Eileen and Tommy Page lived on the edge of the

Charlwood Estate in a block of flats owned by the local housing association. The flat, on the first floor, appeared warm and comfortable and was nicely furnished, but Eileen Page seemed uneasy when she opened the door and invited Rachel into her living room.

'I've been really worried since you phoned,' she said as she indicated for Rachel to sit down on a two-seater settee. 'Oh, I know you said it wasn't anything to worry about, but then you said it was about Tommy and, well, I've worried about Tommy since the day he was born.'

'Oh, Eileen, I'm so sorry,' said Rachel in concern. 'I really didn't mean to alarm you.'

'Is it anything about his health?' Eileen still looked anxious, her forehead furrowed.

'No, it isn't his health.' Rachel shook her head then coming straight to the point she went on, 'I think, Eileen, that Tommy has developed a bit of a crush on me.'

Eileen stared at her. 'Well,' she said, 'I know he's very fond of you—but is that a problem?'

'Not in itself, no, of course it isn't,' Rachel replied. 'But I'm afraid it is getting a bit much, Eileen.'

'In what way? I don't understand.' She frowned.

'Well, it started with a note left at the surgery,' Rachel explained, 'then there were several emails and then this morning there were flowers left for me.'

'And you think all this was Tommy?' Eileen stared at her in amazement.

'Well, I certainly had the feeling that it was Tommy,' Rachel replied. 'He does go out on his own sometimes, doesn't he?'

'Yes, he will go to the shops on his own,' Eileen agreed. 'But he can only usually remember one item at a time. For instance, he will go to the local shop for a newspaper but there wouldn't be any point my asking

him to bring back anything else because he simply
wouldn't remember it.'

'I see,' said Rachel. Taking a deep breath, she went
on, 'Did you say he has access to a computer?'

'Yes, he does,' Eileen agreed. 'The day centre provided one for him and he plays games on it.'

'Does he send emails?' asked Rachel.

'I don't think so—I've never heard him mention
emails,' said Eileen. Looking up quickly, she added, 'I
don't know much about computers but don't you have
to have an address to send someone an email?'

'Yes, that's right,' Rachel said.

'So how would Tommy know yours?'

'I must admit, I have no idea, Eileen,' said Rachel. 'I
only know that, whoever is doing it, I want it to stop
because it's getting a bit disturbing.'

'Yes, I'm sure it is,' Eileen said. She paused.
'Have…have these messages been threatening in any
way?' she asked at last.

'Not really,' Rachel replied. 'Although there was one,
which I replied to, asking who the sender was, and it
came back saying that I know who it is. I just found that
a bit scary really.'

'Oh, dear.' Eileen looked troubled. 'Yes, that is scary.
Look, I'll have a word with Tommy and try to find out
if it is him. But I have to say that somehow I doubt it.
It really sounds like someone who is far more…' She
hesitated as if searching for the right word.

'Sophisticated?' asked Rachel.

'Yes, that's right.' Eileen seized on the word. 'Far
more sophisticated than Tommy. You have to remember,
Doctor, Tommy still has the mind of a child.'

'Yes, Eileen, I know.' Rachel stood up. 'But I would
be very much obliged if you would just have a little

word with him, because if it isn't him, and it goes on, I really do think I'm going to have to report the matter to the police.'

Eileen followed her out to the front door where Rachel paused for a moment, one hand on the catch. 'Oh, there was just one other thing, Eileen,' she said. 'Does Tommy ever go out at night?'

'Hardly ever,' Eileen replied, 'and certainly not on his own.'

'When he does, is he ever picked up by car?'

'Occasionally his cousin will come and collect him and take him down to McDonald's for a meal but that hasn't happened for a long time now.'

'I see. Well, thank you for your help, Eileen.'

Moments later she was driving through the Charlwood Estate back to the medical centre without feeling that she had achieved very much. Maybe Eileen had been telling the truth and Tommy really wasn't capable of the subtlety of her mystery admirer, or perhaps she knew he was and with a mother's instinct she was simply seeking to protect her son. Whatever the reasons, Rachel decided the only thing she could do was to wait and see if anything of a similar nature happened again.

She didn't have long to wait. That afternoon, between patients in her surgery, she checked her emails. Once again there was a message from 'your friend'. Her heart was thumping as she clicked on the 'open' option.

Hello, read the message, *it's me again. Did you like the flowers? Yellow roses are your favourite, aren't they?*

She stared at the message. Probably Eileen wouldn't have had time to talk to Tommy yet—not if he was at his day centre all day. The emailer admitted to being the sender of the flowers but also stated that he knew them to be her favourites. She had been willing to accept that Tommy might have hit on them by a strange coincidence but how could he possibly have known that the flowers were her favourites? So few people knew that. It was disturbing because once again it raised the possibility that her mystery admirer could be someone other than Tommy. And if it wasn't Tommy, she thought, trying to quell a little surge of panic as she gazed at the screen, then who the hell was it?

She had little time for further speculation, however, for as she finished her surgery Julie rang through to ask if she would see an extra patient.

'Who is it, Julie?' she asked. It had been an extremely busy and somewhat stressful day and she had been looking forward to going home, running a relaxing bath and pouring a glass of wine to help herself unwind. It wasn't her turn to take the extra evening surgery for emergencies—maybe this patient would be prepared to see the duty doctor.

Julie's reply swiftly caused her to change her mind. 'It's Rowena Woodhouse,' she said. 'I know you aren't duty doctor tonight, Rachel, but she has particularly asked to see you.'

Rachel had slumped in her chair after the departure of her last patient but she sat up straight now. 'I'll see her, Julie,' she said. 'Send her in now.'

A few moments later Rowena knocked at the door and came into the room. She was not in such a distressed state as she had been the last time Rachel had seen her but, with dark circles under her eyes, she still looked tired and very strained.

'Rowena.' Rachel half rose from her chair and indicated a seat. 'Come in, please, sit down. Now, tell me,' she said as the young woman sat down as if she had in some way been programmed to obey instructions, 'how are you feeling?'

'Numb, really.' Rowena turned dull eyes in Rachel's direction.

'Yes, I'm sure you are.' Rachel nodded. 'I'm afraid we don't have the results of the HIV test yet, they take a bit longer than—'

'That isn't why I'm here,' Rowena interrupted her.

'Oh?'

'There's something I have to tell you,' the woman continued. 'It's something I really should have told the police but I didn't think about it at the time.'

'You don't think you should be telling the police now?' asked Rachel gently.

Rowena shook her head. 'I would rather tell you.'

CHAPTER EIGHT

RACHEL waited, knowing instinctively that Rowena could not be hurried in what she was about to say and at the same time also knowing that, whatever this was, it could be tremendously important and vital to the police investigation.

'I...I should have said before,' said Rowena at last, 'but I was so upset that I didn't really think about it, and then when I did, I didn't think the two things could be connected...not really... And then...' she swallowed '...when I thought about it again...I thought the police probably should know. But I just couldn't face going back there. Then I remembered you and how kind you were to me that night.'

'Is it something else you've remembered?' asked Rachel gently. 'That often happens,' she went on. 'Someone will remember some vital piece of evidence after the event. That's because they are so traumatised when it's actually happening that the memory—'

'It isn't something that happened at the time,' Rowena interrupted her.

'No?' Rachel frowned.

Rowena shook her head. 'It was something that happened before,' she said slowly.

It suddenly felt very still, very quiet, almost as if the very room itself held its breath, waiting to hear what Rowena was about to say. 'Go on,' said Rachel quietly.

'There was this man,' said Rowena at last. When Rachel remained silent, waiting for her to continue, she drew a deep, shuddering breath. 'I first noticed him out-side the library where I work. He just used to stand there on the opposite side of the road, staring in. At first I didn't take too much notice. We have several homeless people who come into the reading room,' she explained. 'It's warm in there—and sometimes they congregate on the steps or in the park opposite.' She swallowed again then continued. 'This particular man eventually started coming in,' she said. She spoke so quietly that Rachel was forced to lean forward in order to hear what she was saying. 'He would sit for hours in the reading section from where he could see me on the desk, and he would just stare.'

'Did you mention this to anyone else?' asked Rachel.

'I told one of my colleagues that I found him a bit unnerving,' Rowena replied, 'but she said he was just a weirdo and to ignore him.'

'And were you able to do that?' Rachel frowned.

'To a point, I suppose.' Rowena gave a slight shrug. 'But then he took to leaving the library when I did and would follow me when I went to get my car. If I hurried he would hurry, that sort of thing.'

'Did he speak to you at all?'

'Yes, one evening he asked me for a lift to the shop-ping precinct.'

'And?' Rachel raised her eyebrows.

'I refused, but he got angry, demanding to know what was wrong with him. He said that he supposed I thought he was a down-and-out but that he wasn't. He said…he said he had a home and that he would show it to me…'

'What happened after that?'

'I was on the point of telling someone—either my boyfriend, which I didn't really want to do because I was afraid he might get involved, or maybe the police, although again I was reluctant to do that because I didn't really think this man was dangerous—a nuisance, maybe, but not dangerous.'

'What happened next?'

'He stopped coming to the library—he just seemed to disappear. I tried to forget about him but then…then…' Rowena gulped and the tears, which Rachel suspected were never far away, sprang to her eyes. 'Do…do you think…?' she said as she dashed the tears away with the back of her hand, 'do you think it was the same man…who…?'

'I don't know, Rowena,' said Rachel gently. Then leaning forward, she took the girl's hands in hers. 'But what I do know is that you have to tell the police.'

'Do I have to?' asked Rowena.

'Yes, you do. It may not be the same man but on the other hand it could well be, and if it is, it means he's still out there and he may well be planning to attack some other poor unsuspecting girl. You suffered terribly, Rowena, but you escaped with your life—the next one may not.' The silence in the room was almost overpowering as Rowena struggled with her emotions.

'Listen,' said Rachel at last, 'if you feel it's too much of an ordeal to go back to the police station, how about if I phone and get someone to come here to the surgery and take your statement?'

Rowena was silent again for a long moment as if she wrestled with dark demons of her own. Then she lifted her head, and as the tears ran unchecked down her face she nodded. 'Yes,' she said at last, 'all right.'

'Good girl,' said Rachel, leaning back and lifting the telephone receiver. 'And don't worry, I'll stay right here with you.'

They put her straight through to Nick this time.

'Nick,' she said not giving him time to express surprise or delight or anything else, 'I need you to come to the surgery.'

'What's the problem?' he asked.

'I have Rowena Woodhouse here,' she said. 'She wants to add to her statement but she doesn't want to go to the station.'

'That's understandable,' said Nick. 'So, this extra information—would you say it's significant?'

'Very,' Rachel replied.

'We're on our way,' said Nick, and the line went dead.

He arrived in less than fifteen minutes accompanied by Terry, and Rachel met them in Reception under the astonished gaze of Danielle and Julie.

'I'll take you up to my consulting room,' said Rachel. 'Rowena is waiting there.'

'Has she remembered something else?' asked Nick as they climbed the stairs.

'Not exactly,' Rachel replied. 'At least, not about the attack itself. What she's saying is that she had received unwanted attentions from a man—a stranger—some while before the attack.'

'This could be significant, Guv,' said Terry, and there was no disguising the edge in his voice, an edge of tension, excitement. By this time they had reached Rachel's consulting room and as they entered Rowena looked up, startled at the appearance of the two detectives even though she'd known they were coming.

'It's all right, Rowena.' Rachel sat down beside her and took her hand. 'I'm going to be right here but I want you to tell DCI Kowalski and DI Payne exactly what you told me just now.'

When Rowena had finished telling her story Rachel

threw a glance in Nick's direction. His expression was unreadable. 'Thank you, Rowena,' he said simply. He was sitting on the edge of a chair and he leaned forward now in order to be able to look into the girl's face. 'Now, tell me, would you be able to give us a description of this man?' he asked.

Rowena nodded. At that moment the intercom buzzed and Rachel answered it. 'Rachel, I'm sorry.' It was Danielle's voice. 'I know you have the police with you but I thought you might want to know that Mrs Woodhouse has just arrived. She's rather anxious about Rowena. She knows she came here to see you but she said she didn't think she would be so long.'

'All right, Danielle, thank you. Tell Mrs Woodhouse that Rowena is perfectly all right and that we'll be down in a moment.' As Rachel replaced the receiver she realised that Nick was still talking to Rowena.

'What we'd really like,' he said, 'would be for you to come down to the station and help us build up a Photofit of this person.'

When Rowena shrank further back into her chair at his words, Rachel intervened. 'Rowena,' she said, 'your mother is downstairs. Apparently she was worried about you. Supposing she was to go with you to the station?'

Still Rowena hesitated. 'We need to pursue this, Rowena,' said Nick gently.

Rowena looked up at Rachel, then Nick, then Terry who stood with his back to the door, 'All right,' she whispered at last. 'I'll do it.'

On the way downstairs Nick took Rachel's arm and squeezed it briefly. 'Thanks,' he said.

'That's OK,' Rachel said, aware once again of the devastating effect his touch seemed to have on her but at the same time not wanting him to suspect as much. 'I hope it will be of some help.'

'Oh, it well might,' he said softly. 'A similar story has come from Kaylee Munns's friends.'

'What do you mean?' She stopped and threw him a startled glance.

He paused on the stairs as well, one hand on the banister. 'It appears that Kaylee had been the victim of a stalker in the weeks leading up to her death. We were beginning to think we were up against a brick wall but this new information could change everything.'

Rowena's mother was waiting in Reception and she stood up as her daughter came down the stairs, accompanied by Rachel and the two men. Briefly Nick explained to her who they were, that he wanted Rowena to go with them to the station and that she wanted her mother to go with her. Together they moved towards the door then Nick turned back to Rachel. 'I'll be in touch,' he said softly, as briefly, for one moment, his gaze met and held hers.

'Yes, all right,' she said, then stood back and watched as the group left the building and headed for the car park.

'Well!' said Danielle as the doors closed behind them. 'That was a bit of excitement, wasn't it? Do you know what it was all about, Rachel?'

'Even if she did, she couldn't tell us,' said Julie, 'so I suggest you get on with the filing.'

'Yeah, I s'ppose,' said Danielle with a huge sigh. 'But I have to say that Rowena Woodhouse looks absolutely terrified.'

'Well, wouldn't you?' said Julie. 'The poor girl was raped and nearly murdered and they still haven't got the bloke that did it.'

'Any more than they've got Kaylee Munns's killer—

I say, do you think it could be the same guy?' Danielle's blue eyes became round.

'Could be, I suppose. I don't know.' Julie shrugged. 'What do you think, Rachel?'

'I've no idea,' said Rachel.

'Well, I don't know what the police are up to,' said Julie with a sniff. 'You'd think they would have caught someone by now, what with all the DNA testing and that they have these days.'

'They have to be absolutely certain before they make an arrest that the evidence will hold up in court,' said Rachel. Suddenly she felt compelled to defend Nick and his team, knowing the hours of painstaking work that was going into their investigation.

'Well, I know one thing for certain,' said Julie with a shudder. 'I won't feel safe until they've got him.'

'Me neither,' added Danielle.

Slowly Rachel made her way back up the stairs to her consulting room where she shut the door behind her and for a few moments leaned against it with her eyes closed. For some reason she had found the events of the last hour incredibly stressful, which was quite ridiculous really when she considered that she of all people should be used to dealing with this sort of thing, not only as a GP but as a doctor assigned to special police duties.

Taking a deep breath, she moved forward and sat down behind her desk. She was about to check her emails when her phone suddenly rang, causing her to jump violently. 'Hello,' she said lifting the receiver to her ear, 'Rachel Beresford.'

'Oh, Dr Beresford—it's Eileen, Eileen Page.'

'Oh, Eileen, hello.' Rachel's fingers tightened around the receiver.

'Doctor, I just thought that you would like to know

that I've spoken to Tommy about the matter we discussed,' said Eileen.

'What did he say, Eileen?' asked Rachel. Suddenly her chest felt extremely tight and she found it difficult to breathe.

'Well, to be perfectly honest with you, Doctor,' Eileen replied, 'he really didn't know what I was talking about. He admitted to liking you but that really was as far as it went. I know Tommy, Dr Beresford, and I know when he is trying to lie to me. He wasn't lying over this, believe me. I don't know who it is who's been sending you those messages and the flowers, but it certainly isn't Tommy.'

'Right, Eileen.' From somewhere Rachel found sufficient breath to reply. 'Well, I'm sorry I bothered you with it. I appreciate what you've done and thank you.'

She hung up and sat for a long time staring out of the window without really seeing what was beyond. So Tommy wasn't her mystery admirer, or at least his mother didn't seem to believe that was the case, and surely Eileen knew him better than anyone? In one way she felt relieved it wasn't Tommy, for if it had been him and if it had gone on, sooner or later she would have had to involve the police. Neither Tommy nor his mother would have coped very well with that. But it still left the question of if it wasn't Tommy, who was it?

Rowena had spoken of being the object of a stalker, and now Nick had said that Kaylee Munns also had received unwanted attention from someone before she'd been murdered. Rachel's stomach churned. Surely her mystery admirer couldn't be the same person?

With fingers that trembled she reached out and clicked her computer mouse to check her emails. For some reason she hadn't really been expecting there to be anything so when she saw that there was one from 'your friend' her heart missed a beat. Taking a deep breath, she opened it.

I saw your boyfriend visiting you the other night, it said. *I don't like that, Rachel.*

She stared at the screen. For the first time there seemed to be an element of threat in the message. If the sender had seen Nick at her house, it must have been him sitting in the parked car…watching. Although she had half wondered about the parked car in the close, she now shivered violently at the very thought.

She had to tell Nick now—there were no two ways about it.

At that moment there came a tap at her door and before she had the chance to call out, Bruce Mitchell put his head round the door. Quickly Rachel deleted the offending email.

'What's going on, Rachel?' asked Bruce, coming right into the room. 'I understand the place is swarming with CID.'

'Not quite.' Rachel managed a weak smile. 'There were two of them here, certainly.'

'So what was it all about?' Bruce frowned.

'The young woman who was raped wanted to add something to her statement and she didn't want to go to the station,' Rachel explained, 'so I asked them to come here instead.'

'This is a nasty business,' said Bruce. 'I shall be glad when it's all over and Westhampstead can get back to normal again. Do you know, the police even called on us last night in their house-to-house investigations?'

'All part of the routine, I suppose,' said Rachel. 'I guess they have to work by a process of elimination.'

'It's a shame you've had all this to cope with since you've been here,' said Bruce, looking at her thoughtfully. 'I can assure you it isn't usually anything like this here.'

'No, Bruce, I know.' Rachel smiled. 'But don't worry about me, it's all in the line of duty.'

Suddenly all she wanted was to go home to the house in Cathedral Close, where she could shut herself in and feel safe. After Bruce had left her consulting room she shut down her computer, stood up and pulled on her jacket before leaving the room and walking downstairs to Reception. 'Goodnight,' she called out to the receptionists and to Patti, who was talking to the two women.

'Goodnight, Rachel,' they chorused.

She crossed the car park to her car and for the first time since all this had happened—the murder, the rape and the strange messages she had been receiving—she found herself looking nervously over her shoulder as she wondered if there might be a connection. And later, after driving home, she found herself checking the close for parked cars, relieved to find there were none.

By the time she was inside and had bolted the door and secured the chain she had convinced herself that the man who had murdered Kaylee Munns, the man who had raped and attempted to murder Rowena Woodhouse and her own mystery admirer were one and the same person, which meant, if this was true, that until this man was caught she was in every bit as much danger as the other two women had been. The fact that the other two had been stalked before the attacks had come as something of a shock but her biggest cause for concern had been finding out that Tommy had not been responsible for the unwanted attention she had been receiving.

She found herself going over and over the sequence of events that had dogged her since her arrival in Westhampstead. First there had been those phone calls where the caller had hung up. She hadn't thought too much of those at the time but now in the light of recent events they became more worrying. Next had come the message left in Reception, the ongoing emails, the car parked outside her house for hours with its silent watcher and, of course, the flowers. Perhaps the flowers had been the most worrying of all, for where at first she had imagined it to be a coincidence that the sender had hit on her favourite flowers, the subsequent email message had shown it was no such thing. Her stalker—for that is what he was, she thought with chilling conviction—knew her and, if the roses were anything to go by, knew her very well.

Nick had known about her love of yellow roses. Nick knew her very well.

It couldn't be Nick. It simply couldn't. She couldn't even contemplate that possibility. But whoever it was also knew her every movement—where she lived, her phone number, her email address…

Round and round her tormented thoughts chased each other throughout that long evening. She attempted to prepare supper for herself, only to eat half of it, the remainder abandoned, swept into the waste bin. She watched television for a while without really knowing what she was watching, agonising over whether she should contact the police and tell them what had been happening to her. The one thing that had prevented her from doing so had been in involving Tommy in some way but even though it now seemed unlikely to have been Tommy, she still didn't want to. Phoning them would somehow make it real, official, and she wasn't sure she was ready to cope with that.

She was still wrestling with indecision when her phone suddenly rang, causing her to jump so violently that she almost upset a mug of coffee that she'd just made for herself.

'Hello?' she said tentatively, half expecting the caller to hang up.

'Rachel, it's Nick.'

'Oh, Nick.' The relief at hearing his voice was overwhelming, overriding those disturbing thoughts she'd had about the possibility of him being her stalker, making her feel guilty at having even thought such a thing.

'I'm sorry it's so late,' he said, 'but can I come and see you?'

'Yes,' she said, 'of course. Where are you?'

'I'm just leaving the station—I could be with you in about ten minutes or so.'

'All right,' she said, 'I'll see you then.'

By the time her doorbell rang she had reached a decision—she would tell Nick everything. What she wasn't prepared for, however, when she opened the door was the expression on his face—one she was at a loss to interpret.

'Nick…?' she said.

'Can we go inside?' he said.

'Of course. Come in.' He stepped into the hall and she closed the door behind him then led the way into the sitting room. 'What's happened?' she asked.

'We've got him,' he said. There was a mixture of emotions in the simple statement—relief, fatigue, satisfaction, triumph even.

'You've…?' Rachel stared at him. 'How? When?'

With a deep sigh Nick almost collapsed onto the sofa while Rachel perched beside him.

'We were almost there,' he said at last. 'We just needed that last vital piece of evidence which today Rowena supplied when she gave us the description of her stalker. Then we assembled the Photo-fit and finally we made our arrest and set up an identity parade.'

'She picked him out?' asked Rachel, almost in amazement.

'Oh, yes, and we've charged him.'

'But that's wonderful! So was it the same man as Kaylee's attacker?'

'Yes.' Nick leaned his head on the back of the sofa and briefly closed his eyes. 'One and the same. Your suggestion of a link with the canal was crucial, Rachel,' he went on after a moment.

'Really?' Her eyes widened.

'Yes, he lives on a run-down old canal boat which has been moored off Millar's Wharf. There's also a possibility he's linked to two other unsolved murders in other towns off the canal. The pattern is always the same—he stalks his victims over a period of time then pounces, rapes and strangles them, only in Rowena's case she got away. The rest will all come out in court but I would say we have enough evidence through DNA and the like to put him away for a very long time. Heaven only knows how many more would have become victims.'

There was a long silence between them where the only sounds in the room were that of the ticking of the clock on the mantelpiece and the distant hum of traffic on the dual carriageway.

'Actually, Nick,' said Rachel and her voice seemed to be coming from a long way off, 'I think I might have been the next one.'

'Sorry?' He'd closed his eyes again but he opened them now and turned his head to look at Rachel. 'The next what?'

Rachel swallowed. 'The next victim,' she said.

'What do you mean?' Frown lines appeared between his eyes.

'I…I've been having rather strange things happen lately,' she said. 'I didn't think too much about them at first but more recently they'd become a little more worrying…'

'What sort of things?' He was alert now, attentive, in policeman mode.

'It started with strange phone calls. You know the sort of thing—I'd pick up the phone and I'd know there was someone there, listening, then they'd hang up without speaking. Then an envelope was handed into the surgery for me, with a handwritten note inside saying, *I love you, Rachel.* Shortly after that the emails started—'

'What sort of emails?' He was definitely in policeman mode now.

'Just chatty sort of things, nothing offensive.'

'Did you reply to them?'

'Once I did,' she admitted. 'I asked who the sender was and the reply came back that I should know who it was.' Rachel took a deep breath and found her hands had started to shake slightly.

Nick must have noticed her distress for he leaned forward and gently touched her arm. 'Take your time,' he said.

'It's all right,' she gulped, 'I'm OK.'

'What happened next?'

'The flowers.'

'Ah, yes,' he said, 'the yellow roses—so did you not find out who sent them?'

She shook her head. 'There was an email, though, asking me if I liked them and making reference to the fact that the sender knew they were my favourite flowers.'

Nick muttered an expletive under his breath. 'Did you reply to that?'

'No.' She shook her head. 'But there's been a car, Nick, a car that I've noticed parked outside here on a couple of occasions late at night, and I think there was someone sitting in the passenger seat as if they were watching the house. And then…' Her voice shook with emotion. 'Then I received another email saying they saw my boyfriend visiting me and that they didn't like that.'

'Your boyfriend?' Nick's frown deepened.

'They must have meant you, when you came here the other night—there hasn't been anyone else here…' Her voice cracked. 'Oh Nick, do you think it was him? Do you think I would have been next?'

'I can hardly believe this, Rachel.' Nick was quite obviously astounded at what he had heard.

'Well, it really happened.'

'I don't doubt that,' he said tersely. 'What I can't believe is that you never told me.'

'There was a reason for that, Nick.'

'I can't imagine what the reason could be.' He still looked astounded.

'I thought I knew who it was,' Rachel faltered.

'So go on.' He stared at her. 'Tell me, who did you think it was?'

'I thought it was a patient.' She took another deep breath. 'A young man called Tommy Page…'

'I know Tommy,' said Nick, 'at least, only so much as to have seen him around the town with his mother. What made you think it was Tommy?'

'I heard him tell his mother one day that he loved me and it was shortly after that the note was handed in at Reception, then the phone calls and the emails…'

'Why the hell didn't you tell me?' There was a mixture of exasperation and anger in Nick's eyes as he looked at her.

'I didn't want to get Tommy into trouble,' she said. 'His mother does a fantastic job looking after him and I just didn't want to add to her worries.'

'And what if it wasn't Tommy? Didn't that occur to you, given what was going on in the town at the same time?' He looked faintly incredulous now, putting Rachel onto the defensive.

'Not at first I didn't, no,' she replied firmly, tilting her chin.

'And afterwards?' He raised one eyebrow.

'Well, yes, I must admit I did begin to doubt it could be Tommy. The things that were happening did seem to be beyond his capabilities...'

'And yet still you didn't tell me?'

'No,' she replied defensively, 'because I still couldn't quite convince myself it wasn't Tommy. So in the end I went to see his mother. Tommy wasn't there, he was at the day centre—anyway, I told his mother what was happening and asked her if she would have a word with him.'

'And what was her reaction to that?' Nick was still very much the policeman.

'She said she would but she also made it plain that she doubted it was Tommy, that basically he wouldn't be capable of it.'

'She could have simply been trying to protect him.'

'Yes, I know,' Rachel said. 'I thought that, too. Anyway, I thought I'd wait and see if anything else happened but then Rowena came to the surgery and told me about her stalker.'

'Did that alert you to the fact that this could have been the same person harassing you?'

'Not immediately, although I have to say I was becoming uneasy by this time, but it wasn't until the last email that I really became concerned.'

'The one about seeing me visiting you?'

'Yes. Oh, Nick,' she said, rising to her feet in sudden agitation and wringing her hands, 'do you really think it was him?'

'I would say there's a very strong possibility,' he admitted. 'We'll question him further obviously but I doubt he'll be very forthcoming.'

'But how would this man have known so much about me?'

'You'd be surprised,' said Nick, looking up at her. 'His type make it their business to find out. Just as he hung about the library finding out as much as he could about Rowena, and apparently following Kaylee Munns and hanging around the stall where she worked in the market and going to the club where she went, so, too, he could have been hanging around the medical centre.'

'That still doesn't explain how he knew about the yellow roses,' said Rachel, 'and my email address—how in the world did he get that?'

Nick stood up. 'Goodness knows,' he said. 'Did you keep the emails?'

'No, I deleted them.'

'We could probably retrieve them from your Internet service provider, but I doubt they would tell us very much. That is if you want us to set up a separate inquiry into this.'

'I don't think there's much point,' said Rachel. 'If it was Tommy then I think now that his mother is involved he will probably stop, and if it was the guy you have in custody I have nothing more to fear.'

'Oh, Rachel.' Nick stared at her, his expression indefinable, then gently he took hold of her shoulders and turned her to face him. 'If only you'd told me.'

'I know,' she whispered. 'I'm sorry, I should have told you, Nick.' She looked up into his face as he let go of her shoulders and slipped his arms around her, holding her tight.

'I don't know what I would have done if anything had happened to you,' he said, and suddenly his voice was husky with emotion. 'I don't think I could have borne it, Rachel, to have found you again after all this time...only to lose you to a perverted fiend like that...'

Rachel had grown very still in his arms, hardly daring to breathe, then as the meaning of his words became clear and the look in his dark eyes echoed the desire that was rising in her own body, she allowed her arms to go around his neck, her fingers to sink into his hair and her lips to part beneath his.

CHAPTER NINE

THIS time there was no holding back. This time all the pent-up passion and frustration that had lain dormant in the years they'd been apart and that had simmered so dangerously near the surface since the moment they had met again suddenly exploded.

'Rachel, oh, my Rachel,' Nick groaned between kisses, kisses so hot, so passionate that Rachel began to fear she might never recover. 'I can't lose you again, not now that I've found you.' His hands moulded her body with a strength that left her gasping.

'I want you, Rachel,' he muttered. 'I love you, I always have.'

Any such explosion of passion had its point of no return and it was Rachel who, when that moment arrived, briefly restrained Nick and held him back.

'Not here,' she whispered. 'Upstairs.'

Their clothes and shoes formed a trail out of the sitting room, through the hall, up the stairs and into her bedroom where at last they both gave in to the overwhelming surge of desire that threatened to consume them.

For Rachel it felt like coming home as memories flooded back and all sensation reached a new heightened level—the sight of him, the feel, the smell were all as she remembered. He had been her first love and all that was different now was the benefit of experience that each had gained in the intervening years. They had both been very young before, young and immature, unsure of themselves, but that had changed now as, with a skill and mastery that took her breath away, Nick made love to her and lifted her to almost forgotten heights of pleasure.

Afterwards they lay in a tangle of bedclothes, satiated and fulfilled.

'That,' said Nick, rolling onto his back and staring up at the ceiling, 'was every bit as good as I remembered—better, in fact, if I'm honest. What do you think?' Turning his head, he looked lazily at Rachel.

'I'll tell you later,' she replied, lifting her arms and stretching luxuriously.

'Later?' He raised himself on one elbow and quizzically looked down at her.

'Yes, if I remember correctly, once was never enough for you—you always wanted seconds. And I have to say I usually found it to be even sweeter the second time around. Unless, of course…'

'Unless what?' he demanded.

'Nothing.' She turned her head away from him but he was not prepared to let her get away with that. With a speed that left her gasping he moved across the bed until his body covered hers once more.

'Now, tell me what you meant,' he said, seizing her wrists and imprisoning them on either side of her head.

'That you might not be up to it now…that's all!' Gasping and laughing, she arched her body against his, trying to twist away from him but failing miserably.

'And whatever makes you think that?' His grip tightened and for a fraction of a second it occurred to Rachel how utterly at his mercy she was.

'Only that you're older now, that's all. In those days you were barely out of your teens…young and incredibly virile…'

'And you don't think that's still the case?' He gazed down at her, a wicked expression in his dangerous dark eyes.

'You'd need to prove it to me…' she began.

'Oh, I intend to,' he murmured in the seconds before his mouth claimed hers again, silencing her. 'Make no mistake about that.'

Early morning sunlight flooded the room and Rachel opened her eyes, turned her head and smiled dreamily as she saw the empty space beside her and remembered. Nick had left around five o'clock, stumbling around the room gathering up his clothes, stubbing his toe against the bed, cursing under his breath, taking a shower and dressing, then, pausing only to kiss her goodbye, leaving the house to get himself home to change before work.

It had been wonderful, there was no denying that, she thought as she turned onto her back and gazed up at the patterns of sunlight on the ceiling, but, then, that was hardly surprising for sex between them had always been wonderful. It had been other things that had caused problems—things like parental influence, being apart and Nick's apparent inability to commit. The latter, she now recognised, probably had had something to do with how young they had both been at the time, but it still didn't alter the fact that he had unceremoniously dumped her without so much as an explanation.

Last night he'd said he loved her. Had he meant it or had it been simply a figure of speech, used in the heat of the moment? And what of her—did she still love him, and if she didn't how could she have been so weak as to allow last night to happen? And what about Jeremy? A stab of guilt shot through her. If she was completely honest, she'd totally forgotten Jeremy. And if that was

the case, surely she should be looking at ways of finally
ending the rather tenuous relationship she still had with
him. Even as she lay there and thought about it, she
knew that was what had to happen. She didn't love
Jeremy any more and she had certainly never loved him
in the way she had loved Nick—last night had shown
her that—but how could she be sure that her and Nick
had any sort of future together?

The fact was, of course, that she couldn't be sure of
any such thing. One night of unbridled passion didn't
really prove anything, but the one thing it had shown
her was that, even if this came to nothing with Nick, she
couldn't continue her relationship with Jeremy.

The whole of Westhampstead was agog with the news
that the police had made an arrest in connection with
Kaylee Munns's murder and the rape and attempted murder of Rowena Woodhouse and that a man had been
charged.

'He'd been living in an old boat down on the canal
and stalking local women,' said Julie with a shudder.
'Honestly, it makes your blood run cold just to think
about it.'

It was later that same morning and the staff of the
medical centre had congregated in the staffroom before
opening the doors to the public.

'Well, let's hope they lock him up and throw away
the key,' said Patti, 'not that that will be much help to
the families he's torn apart.'

'Maybe not,' said Bruce, 'but at least when he's con-
victed it will bring about some sort of closure for them,
and for the rest of us, well, perhaps we can slowly get
back to some sort of normality.'

They all filed out of the staffroom and Rachel made

her way up to her consulting room where as a matter of habit she checked her emails. Just for a moment she found herself holding her breath that there might be a message from her mystery 'friend', then with a surge of relief she reminded herself that wouldn't happen any more, only in the next moment to be seized by a dreadful feeling of panic as once again she allowed her mind to go briefly down the avenue of speculation. It now seemed certain that her stalker was the man who had been charged with those other more serious crimes. What if Rowena hadn't come forward when she had, providing that crucial piece of evidence that had led to his arrest? What if he'd remained free? How soon would it have been before he'd made some other sort of contact with her beyond emails? How soon before he would have followed her home, or perhaps lain in wait for her somewhere, pouncing on her in the dark and attacking her? She could hardly bear to think of it even now, and she wasn't certain she would be able to tell anyone else of her fears. She'd told Nick, that was enough. He'd been angry that she hadn't told him before and had reacted by demonstrating how much she meant to him, but the fear was over now and she knew she had to try to put the whole thing out of her mind and get on with her life.

Nick phoned her later that morning and they agreed to meet for a quick lunchtime drink in a coffee-shop in town. Rachel reached the shop first and was sitting at a table in a little alcove towards the rear when Nick arrived. She was amused to see that he looked a bit sheepish and not a little tired as he slipped into the opposite chair.

'Are you angry with me?' he asked at last after the waitress had brought them coffee and blueberry muffins.

'Why should I be angry with you?' She raised her eyebrows.

He shrugged. 'I just thought you might be. I…I hadn't planned for that to happen last night…it just sort of did, that's all.'

'You can't beat a bit of spontaneity,' said Rachel, stirring her coffee.

'Probably not,' Nick agreed, and Rachel smiled to see he looked relieved.

'I thought you might be thinking that I took advantage of the situation,' he said after a moment.

'It could be argued that I did the same,' she replied coolly.

'Well, whatever.' Nick raised his hands in a gesture of surrender. 'I think we were both taken unawares by the strength of emotion.' He paused, staring reflectively into his cup for a moment, then, without looking up, he said, 'What I'm not sure about is where we go from here.'

'Good point,' Rachel agreed. 'I'm not sure either.'

'It's what you want to happen,' Nick went on. 'I'm well aware that it's different for you than for me.'

'In what way?' She frowned slightly.

'Well, I'm unattached,' he replied, 'although having said that anyone who takes me on has to take Lucy as well, but you, well, you are already in a relationship—'

'Nick, we need to talk, I know that,' said Rachel interrupting him. 'I don't mean just like this, here over a cup of coffee, but properly, at length. Our relationship failed once. We need to recognise why and to make sure that if we were to try again the same thing wouldn't happen.'

'Fair enough,' he said agreeingly, 'and you're right— this is neither the time nor the place.' He glanced at his watch. 'In fact, I have to get back very soon. You wouldn't believe the amount of paperwork that is generated by a case like this.'

'I can believe it,' Rachel replied dryly. 'My job is very much the same. And, yes, you're right, there isn't time now to discuss all we need to.'

'I just wanted to see you,' said Nick. As he spoke he reached out across the table and covered her hand with his, his gaze meeting hers.

'I know,' she said softly. 'I wanted to see you as well.'

'I needed to prove to myself that I hadn't dreamt last night.' His dark eyes suddenly sparkled with amusement.

'Well, if you did,' she replied, 'I was in the same dream.'

They parted soon after that with a promise that they would meet soon to discuss the future.

The next few days were incredibly busy, however, leaving Rachel little time to think about her personal life, let alone do anything about sorting it out. Then, one afternoon when she was about to conduct an antenatal clinic, she was waylaid by Julie who told her that her appointment had come through to see a gynaecologist.

'That's good, Julie,' Rachel replied. 'And don't worry, we'll soon find out if there's any reason why you haven't been able to conceive. If there is, hopefully it can be put right and then it will be you attending my antenatal clinic.'

'Oh, I hope so, Rachel,' said Julie fervently, 'I do hope so.'

The clinic went on until quite late in the afternoon and Rachel had only just returned to her room when Julie rang through to say there was a gentleman in Reception, asking to see her.

It was Nick, thought Rachel with a stab of excitement. She hadn't seen him since their snatched lunchtime drink a few days before, though he had phoned her on a couple of occasions, late at night, promising that he would see her again soon. Quickly she left her consulting room and almost ran down the stairs, so great was her haste to see him again. When she reached Reception, however, the man who turned from the window to greet her wasn't Nick at all.

'Jeremy!' she exclaimed, stopping dead in her tracks in shock. 'Whatever are you doing here?'

'Well, that's a fine greeting, I must say,' he said. 'I just thought I'd pay you a surprise visit, that's all. Isn't that allowed?'

'We said no contact...' Rachel began, but, aware of the curious glances from the staff, she swiftly checked herself. 'But now that you're here...' Reaching up, she kissed him on the cheek.

An hour later they were sharing a meal together at the house in Cathedral Close.

'Were you intending to stay?' Rachel asked a little uncertainly.

'No,' he replied, without looking at her. 'I have to go back tonight.'

'It's a long way to come just to say hello and to have supper.'

'Yes,' he agreed. 'Actually, Rachel,' he went on after a moment, 'I don't think this is working. Do you?'

'What isn't working?' She stared at him, wondering what he meant. Ever since he had arrived she had found herself wondering what she had ever seen in him and what was the best and kindest way to tell him that she no longer wanted to continue with their relationship.

'This trial separation,' he said.

Oh, God, she thought wildly, he wants me to go back to him now. What in the world can I say to him to let him down lightly?

'Really, I don't think it was a very good idea in the first place,' he went on.

'Maybe not, but—'

'No, please, Rachel, let me finish. Either a relationship is over or it isn't. A trial separation is a foolish idea that merely prolongs the agony of splitting up, and prevents the couple concerned from getting on with their lives.'

'Well, yes,' she agreed, then stared at him, seeing his expression change and noting that he seemed to have difficulty looking her in the eye. Knowing him as well as she did, she said, 'You've met someone else, haven't you, Jeremy?'

'Well, not exactly that,' he hedged, running one finger around the inside of his collar, 'but I have to say it would be nice to think that if I wanted to ask someone out I could do so without feeling guilty…'

'You've met someone else,' she repeated.

He stared at her then his shoulders slumped slightly. 'Well, actually yes,' he said at last. 'There is someone I'd like to go out with. She—'

'It doesn't matter, Jeremy,' Rachel said weakly, 'it really doesn't.'

'No?' he said uncertainly.

'No.' She shook her head. 'Because I think you are absolutely right. This trial separation thing was a bad idea, we should have had the courage to call it a day.'

'I'm sorry, Rachel, really I am. We had some good times, didn't we?'

'Yes, Jeremy, we did,' Rachel agreed, and to her faint surprise she found that she meant it. 'But…don't feel badly about wanting to move on, because I want to do the same.'

'You do?' He stared at her for a long moment then he frowned. 'Is it your policeman?' he said at last.

'What makes you ask that?' Rachel's eyes widened slightly in surprise.

'Just a hunch,' he said. 'You told me once that you'd had a relationship when you were living at home with a guy who went on to become a policeman, then when we talked on the phone that night you said the local DCI was picking you up to take you somewhere or other—I just wondered, that's all.'

'It may not come to anything, Jeremy,' she said guardedly. 'It's sometimes a mistake to try to go back.'

'Maybe.' He shrugged. 'On the other hand, if you don't give these things a try, I guess you'll never know.'

'You've done *what?*' Georgie stared at Rachel in astonishment. It was the following morning, a Saturday and Rachel's day off, and she'd walked over to the Reynolds' home, where she'd found Georgie in the garden, raking leaves.

'I've finished with Jeremy,' Rachel repeated, 'although, technically, I suppose I should say he finished with me first.'

'For goodness' sake!' Georgie collapsed in a heap on a wrought-iron garden seat and stared up at Rachel as if she could hardly believe what she was hearing. 'Whatever happened?'

'He came to see me—last night,' Rachel replied, perching beside Georgie on the seat. 'It was strange really because I'd already made up my mind to finish the relationship but he beat me to it. He said he thought the trial separation was neither one thing nor the other and he couldn't see much point in going on with it. What he really meant was that he's met someone else.'

'So what did you say?'

'I agreed with him,' Rachel replied with a shrug. 'Then I made him feel even better by going on to say that I had also found someone I wanted to go out with.'

'No need to ask who that is,' said Georgie with a sudden chuckle.

'Yes, well.' Rachel shrugged again, then, seeing Georgie's expression, she gave a rueful smile. 'You were quite right, Georgie—I was besotted with Nick Kowalski once, a long time ago, and really nothing seems to have changed.'

'And what about him?' asked Georgie curiously. 'Does he feel the same way?'

'I think so, yes.'

'You don't sound too sure.' Georgie frowned.

'If I'm really honest, there's still a part of me that's urging caution,' said Rachel. 'I think it has something to do with the way he just dumped me before without a word of explanation. I suppose I'm afraid that if he did it once he could do it again.'

'You have to talk to him about this, Rachel,' said Georgie emphatically, 'you really do. You were both very young when this happened—maybe he thought he was too young for a long-term relationship, or maybe there was some other explanation, but you'll never know unless you ask him and give him a chance to explain.'

'No, I guess you're right.' Rachel paused, reflecting for a long moment, then she looked up again and she said, 'But that wasn't the only reason I came over.'

'No?' Georgie looked up quickly,

'I came to tell your dad that I've had a call from Edward Drummond's secretary to say they've had a cancellation next Tuesday so he'll be able to go and have an angiogram and echocardiogram then.'

'That's wonderful, Rachel.' There were sudden tears in Georgie's eyes. 'But, please, tell me again, what exactly are these tests for?'

'Well, the angiogram lets us see if there are any blockages in the arteries and the echocardiogram lets us listen more fully to the heartbeat.'

'And if there is a problem,' asked Georgie anxiously, 'if the arteries are blocked, what then?'

'There is a procedure called angioplasty where a balloon is passed through the arteries and a stent put in to keep them open,' Rachel explained. 'If that fails, there is always a bypass operation, but let's not jump the gun here. Let's get the tests done first.'

'Thank you, Rachel,' said Georgie. 'You've been so good to Dad.'

'Not at all, it's all part of the service. Now, let's go and tell him, shall we?'

When Rachel left the Reynolds' after talking to Harvey and reassuring him, she decided on a sudden impulse to walk across the park to the new complex of flats where Nick had told her he lived. She didn't for one moment imagine he would be there—no doubt he was working, or if he did have some rare time off then he would probably be planning to spend it with Lucy.

It was a glorious morning. A mist, which had lingered, had cleared to reveal a cloudless blue sky against which the trees, resplendent in their autumn finery, were etched with fine delicacy. Underfoot the fallen leaves were damp with dew while the shrubbery was festooned with spiders' webs that glittered in the sunlight.

To Rachel's surprise Nick opened the door almost immediately after she'd rung the bell. There was no dis-

guising the astonished delight on his face when he saw
her there. 'Rachel!' he exclaimed. 'I had a feeling this
was going to be my lucky day—now I know it is.' He
was casually dressed in sweatshirt and jeans and his feet
were bare, his hair wet as if he'd just stepped out of the
shower.

'Nick, I'm sorry to turn up unannounced…'

'Not at all—come in.' He stood aside to enable her to
enter the hallway of his apartment. 'To what do I owe
the pleasure?' he asked softly as she brushed past him.

'I…I wanted to talk to you,' she said, 'to tell you
something and…to ask you something as well.' A delicious aroma of freshly brewed coffee filled the air and
she lifted her head instinctively. 'That smells good,' she
said.

'I've just made it,' he said. 'Come through to the
kitchen.'

She followed him into a sunny room that overlooked
the canal and was connected through an archway to the
main living area of the apartment. 'This is nice,' she
said, looking around.

'Well, it suits my purpose, at least for the time being,'
he said as he lifted two mugs from a cupboard and set
them on a tray.

'I thought you might be at work today,' she said,
watching him pour the coffee into the mugs.

'Don't you think I've earned a day off?' He grinned.

'Well, yes, but…' She trailed off then said, 'And then
I wondered if you had Lucy with you.'

'I'm seeing her later on.' Lifting the tray, he added,
'Let's take these through and sit in the window.'

She followed him into the living area where he placed
the tray on a pine table in the bay window. They both
sat down on canvas director-style chairs and Rachel

leaned forward to admire the view of the canal. 'This is a glorious spot,' she said, as a brightly painted canal boat drifted slowly past the window. 'It's hard to believe now that the canal was the scene of such violence…'

'That's true,' Nick agreed. Leaning back in his chair, he said casually, 'You haven't had any more messages or anything, have you?'

'No, nothing—but, then, I wouldn't, would I, if this is the same guy?' She paused. 'You *do* think it's the same guy, don't you, Nick?' she added anxiously.

'Yes, he's not admitting anything, but everything points to it being him.'

'Was he the man in the red bandana?' asked Rachel tentatively.

'We think so.' Nick nodded, his expression grim. 'A red scarf was found on his houseboat.'

'Poor Kaylee.' Rachel shook her head. 'It hardly bears thinking about.'

'Rachel…' Nick leaned forward slightly. 'I'm pretty certain it won't happen because, as I say, everything points to him being our man, but if you do get any other communication of any sort I want you to ring me immediately—do you understand that?'

'Yes, of course I do.' She was silent for a while, cradling the mug of coffee in her hands, warming them. The only sounds were those of ducks on the towpath below the window and the faint sound of music being played in another apartment.

'You said you had something to tell me,' said Nick at last, 'and something to ask me.'

'Yes,' she said slowly, 'that's true, I do.' She paused, reflectively staring at the coffee in her cup, then, looking up again, she said, 'I've had a visit from Jeremy.'

His eyes widened. 'When was this?' he asked.

'Last night,' she replied. 'It was just a fleeting visit. He came down to tell me that he didn't think the trial separation is working and that he thought we should end it.'

'He wants you to go back to him.' Nick's voice was dull, devoid of emotion, but the expression that crossed his features was one of pain.

'No,' Rachel replied, 'quite the opposite really. He wants to be free so that he can get on with his life, as he put it, which I rather gathered means he wants to go out with someone else.'

Nick stared at her. 'And how did you feel about that?' he asked softly.

'He did me a favour, actually,' Rachel replied, 'because I'd already decided I was going to end our relationship. There was no point going on with it, Nick, it really had run its course.'

'So that presumably leaves you free as well—to get on with your life,' said Nick, and there was a catch of excitement in his voice now.

'Yes,' she agreed, 'I guess it does.'

'So…?' He hesitated and looked at her.

'I said there was something I wanted to ask you as well,' said Rachel slowly.

'Yes,' Nick agreed, 'yes, you did.'

Rachel swallowed, for some reason nervous now that it had come to the point, maybe a little afraid at what she might hear, what Nick's reasons had been for ending their relationship without so much as a word of explanation. 'It's about us…before…' she said at last.

'What about us…before?' His eyes narrowed slightly.

'About how it ended.'

'I must admit I've wondered about that as well.'

'What I don't understand is why you ended it without any explanation—'

'Why *I* ended it?' He stared at her.

'Yes, Nick,' she said, 'you…just stopped writing. I…I didn't know what to think.'

'Well, did you expect me to go on writing?' His eyes widened slightly. 'I mean, you made it very clear that we were finished, that you'd met someone else, that you'd fallen in love and that you no longer wanted to hear from me.'

'What?' Rachel stared at him in astonishment. 'I don't know what you're talking about,' she said at last. 'I never told you that I'd met someone else and I certainly never said we were finished or that I didn't want to hear from you again.'

He was frowning now, the dark brows drawn tightly together. 'But you put it all in the letter,' he said.

'Letter? What letter?' she asked in bewilderment.

'The last letter you ever wrote to me, of course,' he said, and there was exasperation in his voice now. 'You wrote saying it was all over.'

'Nick, I didn't,' Rachel protested. 'I swear I never wrote any such letter.'

'But it was from you…your handwriting…'

'But I didn't write it!' she declared.

'Then who did?' asked Nick quietly.

'I've no idea,' said Rachel, 'but it certainly wasn't me—why, I was heartbroken when you suddenly stopped writing.'

'Yet you didn't try to contact me to find out why?'

'I waited for a few weeks,' she said slowly, 'then…then I phoned and asked my mother if she'd seen you. She asked me why I wanted to know and I said I hadn't heard from you. She said that she'd seen you around the town with somebody else. I assumed that was why you'd stopped writing—that you'd met someone else. Were you seeing someone else as quickly as that?' she demanded suddenly.

'Of course not!' he retorted. 'I was devastated when you chucked me—that was probably just your mother making sure we didn't take up with each other again. She never did like me, Rachel. I bet she couldn't believe her luck when you told her that I'd stopped writing to you…unless, of course…'

'Unless what?' said Rachel sharply. 'You're not suggesting it was my mother who wrote that letter to you?'

Nick shrugged. 'I'm not suggesting anything, Rachel, but the fact remains, someone wrote it, and it wasn't you.'

'She wouldn't, Nick,' Rachel cried passionately. 'I'm sure she would never have done anything like that. Oh, I know she didn't approve of me going out with you, but she would never have gone to those lengths to stop it. Look, I'll ask her if you like, although I doubt she'd even know what I'm talking about, given the way she is now.'

Nick took a deep breath. 'Does it matter now?' he said at last. 'Does any of it matter? After all, we've found each other again, haven't we?' He stood up and, moving forward until he was standing directly in front of Rachel, held out his hands. When she lifted her own hands he took them in his and drew her to her feet. Looking deeply into her eyes, he said, 'And we *have* found each other again, haven't we?'

'Yes, Nick,' she said softly, 'oh, yes, of course we have. But when I think of all that time we've missed…'

'I know, I know,' he murmured as he dropped small kisses first on her forehead, then her cheek, her eyelids and then more lingeringly on her mouth, 'but doesn't that just mean we have a lot of serious catching up to do?'

'Yes,' she said with a little sigh, 'yes, I guess it does.' But while the prospect of that lay tantalisingly on the horizon Rachel still felt she wanted to know who had been responsible for Nick and her parting in the way they had.

'I always say there's no time like the present, especially when it comes to making up for lost time,' said Nick, as he kissed the warm hollow of her throat.

'That may be so,' replied Rachel, 'but aren't you supposed to be seeing Lucy?'

'Not until later,' he said, his arms tightening around her, 'and I'm hoping that'll you'll join us. It's essential to me that you and Lucy get to know one another.'

'Of course I will,' she said. 'There's nothing I would like better.'

'Wonderful,' he said, 'but that still gives us a couple of hours…'

CHAPTER TEN

THEY picked Lucy up from her mother's at two o'clock. Marilyn came out to the gate and eyed Rachel warily but Lucy bounded happily into the car.

'Marilyn,' said Nick, 'you remember Rachel?'

'Of course,' Marilyn replied and it crossed Rachel's mind that she'd said it as if she, Rachel, was someone she was hardly likely to forget.

'Rachel is in practice at the medical centre for a while,' Nick went on doggedly, as if he was fully aware of the rather frosty reception from his ex-wife but was not going to let it faze him in any way. 'Lucy met her at the Michaelmas Fair—didn't you, Luce?' He half turned to his daughter who was securing her seat-belt in the rear seat of the car.

'Yes,' she said, 'I did. Hi, Dr Beresford.'

'Hello, Lucy,' Rachel replied. Lowering her head so she could see Marilyn through the open window, she added, 'Hello, Marilyn. Long time no see. How are you?'

'I'm fine, thanks,' Marilyn replied. Speaking to Nick again, she said, 'Geoff and I are going shopping but we'll be home around six.'

'Well, I was hoping Lucy could have a meal with us,' Nick replied.

'I don't know about that…' Marilyn began, but it was Lucy herself who put paid to any further discussion.

'Oh, yes,' she cried, 'yes, please. I can, can't I, Mum? Please?'

'Well, yes, I suppose so.' Marilyn sounded reluctant. 'But I want her back by nine.'

'OK,' said Nick lightly, 'nine o'clock it will be.'

There was no discussion about Marilyn between Nick and Rachel, not with Lucy there, but Rachel rather suspected there might be at a later time when they were alone. If what Nick had told her previously was correct, Marilyn had resented Rachel's presence in Nick's life in the past, and even though since then things had altered radically there was still the possibility she might harbour the same feelings. But, thought Rachel as they drove into town, Marilyn had more than had her chance with Nick and it certainly wasn't Rachel's fault that their marriage had failed.

They took Lucy tenpin bowling and for the first time Rachel really came to understand just how much this one small girl meant to Nick and likewise how much Nick meant to Lucy. After the bowling Nick bought huge ice-creams for everyone, then they returned to his apartment and he made spaghetti Bolognese for supper.

'I didn't know you could cook,' said Rachel, as she helped clear the dishes while Lucy curled up on the sofa, watching a favourite film.

'I suspect there may be many things about me you don't know,' he said softly, 'but, hey, it could be great fun finding out.'

'Lucy's a lovely child,' said Rachel.

'I'm so glad you two like each other,' said Nick as he loaded the dishwasher.

'Did I detect a certain frostiness from Marilyn?' Rachel spoke quietly so that Lucy wouldn't hear.

'Maybe.' Nick shrugged. 'But she'll just have to get used to it. She is rebuilding her life, she must be prepared for me to do the same.'

'Nick,' Rachel began hesitantly, 'I've been wondering…'

'Yes, I know,' he said. 'So have I. About that letter?'

'Yes, it's bugging me,' Rachel replied. 'Could it…could it have been…?'

'Marilyn?' he asked, raising his eyebrows. When Rachel nodded, he went on, 'I know, I wondered the same thing, but somehow I can't quite see it.'

'You said yourself that she'd always had a crush on you,' said Rachel slowly. 'Maybe she thought if I wasn't on the scene…?'

'Possibly.' Nick shrugged again. 'But I really don't think so. How would she have been able to copy your handwriting so exactly? Remember, I'd been receiving letters from you for some time and this one certainly had me fooled, so on the face of it I would say it had to be someone who knew you very well.'

'That's the detective in you talking,' she teased with a smile. Growing serious again, she said, 'But from what you say, it does sound unlikely to have been Marilyn. I would like to know who it was, though,' she said after a moment.

'I know,' he agreed. 'So would I. Whoever it was has a lot to answer for.'

'I'm having lunch with my parents tomorrow,' said Rachel slowly. 'If I get the chance I may mention it to my father.'

'Would he have known, though, if it was your mother?' asked Nick doubtfully.

'Only if she told him,' Rachel replied, 'and that is the only way we would find out for certain, because it's very unlikely she is able to remember.'

'Don't upset her, Rachel,' said Nick. 'It's not worth it now, after all this time.'

'No, probably not.' Rachel gave a sigh. 'I can't help agreeing with you, though, that whoever it was certainly has a lot to answer for.'

Nick nodded then glanced at his watch. 'It's a quarter to nine,' he said. 'I have to get Lucy home.'

'And I should be going.'

'Can't you stay a while? I won't be long.' Reaching out his hand he gently touched her cheek, the gesture somehow both tender and exciting.

'Do you realise I've been out since very early this morning?' she protested with a little laugh.

'Then a couple more hours won't make much difference,' he replied, the expression in his eyes leaving no doubt as to the meaning of his words.

'All right,' she said softly. 'I'll stay awhile.'

'Wonderful,' he said. 'I'll be right back.'

'So is it young Kowalski?' It was the following day and Rachel was at her parents' home, having just enjoyed a Sunday lunch cooked by her father. Her mother had been even more vague and forgetful than usual and had retired to her bedroom for a rest. Rachel and her father were sitting in the conservatory at the rear of Ashton House and Rachel had just told him that her relationship with Jeremy was at an end.

'I think it could well be,' Rachel replied carefully in answer to her father's question, 'but it wasn't only that. Jeremy also has someone else. But, yes, you're right, I am seeing Nick.'

'I'm not surprised,' her father replied, 'after seeing the two of you together at the fair.'

'I think really, Daddy, Nick has always been the one.'

'Yes,' he agreed slowly, 'I dare say you're right.'

There was a long silence between them as Rachel

geared herself up to ask the inevitable question. 'You know…' she began at last, 'you know when Nick and I parted before…?'

'Yes.' Her father nodded. 'Didn't you say he ended it soon after you went to medical school?'

'I did,' she agreed, 'at least that's what I thought, but, in fact, things were a bit different. You see, it appears he received a letter which he believed to be from me, telling him that our relationship was over because I had met and fallen in love with someone else. The thing is, Daddy…' she took a deep breath '…I never wrote any such letter. But Nick thought I had, and so he stopped writing to me.'

'That's strange, isn't it?' Her father frowned. 'But didn't you try to contact him to find out why he had stopped writing?'

'No,' Rachel replied, 'because when I spoke to Mummy about it and told her that he had stopped writing, she told me that she had seen him with someone else. After that, I believed he had ended the relationship without a word of explanation because he *had* met someone else.'

'It's all sounding a bit complicated,' said James, scratching his head.

'Not really, Daddy,' said Rachel. 'What it boils down to is that Nick and I parted because of whoever it was who wrote that letter.'

Her father was silent for a moment then, casting her a sidelong glance, he said, 'Any ideas as to who it might have been?'

'Nick says it must have been someone who knew me very well to have been able to imitate my handwriting so perfectly.'

Her father stared at her in the silence that followed

then slowly he said, 'Rachel, you're not thinking…that this might have been your mother, are you?'

'I don't know what to think, Daddy.' Rachel shook her head. 'It had to be someone who wanted us to part and Mummy had always made it very plain that she didn't like Nick—and she *was* very relieved when we split up. She also told me he was seeing someone else when in actual fact he wasn't…so…'

'She wouldn't, Rachel,' her father replied firmly. 'She would never have done anything like that—she would have looked on it as forgery and you know how she feels regarding the letter of the law. And in those days she was a magistrate…'

'Well, that's what I thought—' Rachel began, but her father interrupted her.

'Besides,' he said, 'if she had done anything like that she would have told me. Oh, she might not have told me at the time but it would have come out later, maybe at the time of young Kowalski's marriage. So, no, Rachel, I'm ninety-nine per cent certain that this had nothing to do with your mother. And as for the other one per cent, well, I'm afraid with the way your mother is now, I can never pursue it.'

'I wouldn't want you to.' Rachel reached out and touched his arm. 'You've got quite enough on your plate as it is.' She paused. 'You *are* coping all right, aren't you?' she added anxiously.

'For the moment, yes.' He nodded.

'And when things get worse, I'll make sure you have help,' Rachel said firmly.

'What about you?' he went on after a moment. 'How are you liking all this police work?'

'I enjoy police work,' Rachel replied. 'I always have.'

'There's been a bit more excitement round here just lately than there usually is,' her father observed.

'You can say that again,' said Rachel lightly. She hadn't told him about the fact that she also might have been in danger. She hadn't wanted to worry him and now that the danger was past she didn't feel there was any need to mention it.

She left Ashton House shortly after that and returned to her own home. Nick, she knew, was on duty that day but later that night she phoned him at home and told him what her father had said.

'He was pretty certain it couldn't have been my mother,' she said. 'And really I'm relieved. I didn't want it to have been her and deep down I didn't really think she would have done such a thing. On the other hand, I would still very much like to know who did write it.'

'You know, Rachel,' he said, 'we may never know.'

'You're probably right.'

'And maybe now that we've found each other again it doesn't matter,' he said softly.

'No,' she agreed, 'maybe it doesn't.'

The following day was incredibly busy, as Mondays in any health centre very often were. In reception the staff were stretched to their limits after Philip Newton phoned in to say that Julie was sick and wouldn't be in for a couple of days. Rachel had a full morning surgery, followed by house visits, then a working lunch combined with a staff meeting. During the meeting Bruce mentioned a sales pitch from a pharmaceutical company that was coming via email concerning drugs and care for patients with Alzheimer's disease.

'I'll check that out,' said Rachel to Bruce as they left

the room together. 'There might be something new to help my mother.'

When she reached her consulting room and clicked the button to receive emails there was indeed one from the drug company, but it was forgotten in the shock she felt when she saw there was also one from 'your friend'.

For a moment she simply stared at the screen in disbelief. It couldn't be, she thought, it simply couldn't. The man was in police custody, awaiting trial for heaven's sake. Surely there was no way he would have access to a computer? With a hand that shook she opened it. The message, stark and clear, was chilling in its simplicity. *I'm still here*, it read. *I bet you thought I'd gone.*

Immediately Rachel picked up the phone, dialled the number of police headquarters and asked to be put through to DCI Kowalski. She was told that he was out on a case but that she could leave a message on his voicemail, which he picked up at frequent intervals. 'Nick,' she said after the tone, 'it's Rachel. I thought you should know I've had another email. It says; ''I'm still here. I bet you thought I'd gone''. It's given me the jitters, Nick, I don't mind telling you. Perhaps you could give me a ring when you get this message.'

Rachel found it incredibly difficult to concentrate during her afternoon surgery and by four o'clock, when Nick still hadn't phoned back, she felt quite nauseous. She had been careful to save the email this time and not delete it, knowing that Nick would want to see it. As she was showing the last patient to the door her phone suddenly rang and she grabbed it, thinking it was Nick, but it was Danielle.

'Rachel, I've got Philip on the phone,' she said. 'He's very worried about Julie. He's asking if you could visit.'

'Did he say what's wrong?' asked Rachel.

'Pain in her stomach, he said,' Danielle replied.

'All right, Danielle,' Rachel replied. 'Put him through, I'll speak to him.' She waited then as she heard the click of the line she said, 'Philip?'

'Rachel?'

'Yes, what's the problem with Julie?'

'She's in a lot of pain, Rachel. She thought it was period pain at first but she says now that it's much worse than that.'

'Has her period started, Philip?'

'Just a moment, I'll ask her.'

There was silence for a few moments then he was back. 'No,' he said, 'she says not but that the pain is really bad now.'

'All right, Philip—tell her to stay in bed and to keep warm and I'll be over shortly.'

After hanging up, Rachel stood up, slipped on her jacket, picked up her case and her car keys and left her room. In the corridor she met Bruce and together they made their way to Reception.

'Hello?' he said on seeing her case. 'Call out?'

'Yes, to Julie, actually.'

'Our Julie?' Bruce raised his eyebrows and when Rachel nodded in reply he said, 'What's the problem?'

'Not sure—abdominal pain, her husband said. I know they've been trying for a baby for some time now but without success, and I've referred her to gynae—but I'm a bit concerned this could be an ectopic pregnancy.'

'I'll let you get on, then,' said Bruce. As they reached Reception, he said, 'Oh, did you get the Alzheimer's email?'

Rachel paused. Why was he asking her that? 'Yes,' she said, 'but I haven't had the chance to check it yet.'

On the way to her car she found herself wondering if it could be Bruce who had been responsible for the emails. Then she dismissed the thought—she really was becoming paranoid now, she told herself firmly as she started the engine. Why, at one time there she had even suspected Nick—as if it could have been him.

But…the little voice of reason niggled at the back of her mind, it *had* to be someone. At least it wasn't the stalker—the murderer, she reminded herself. He was safely locked up—there was no way she was in any danger from him. It was far more likely that her first suspicions had been correct and it was indeed Tommy who had a fixation about her and who was obviously capable of far more than he led his mother to believe.

There was a light drizzle, enough to need to use the windscreen wipers, and the low cloud made the late afternoon seem darker than it really was, while the canal, when Rachel reached it, appeared deep, gun-metal grey. The Newtons lived in a cul-de-sac of modern, semi-detached houses built of yellow brick, and Rachel found number eleven with no trouble and parked outside. The garden had a small lawn surrounded by neat flower-beds filled with wallflowers and yellow and white chrysanthemums, and after Rachel had rung the doorbell the door was opened almost immediately by Philip.

'Oh, Rachel,' he said, 'it's so good of you to come.' Rachel noticed he looked agitated and there was a bead of sweat on his upper lip. 'Come in,' he added, standing back for her to enter the small hallway.

'Hello, Philip,' she said stepping inside. 'How is she?'

'She's in a lot of pain,' he replied. 'She's in bed, like you said.' He indicated the stairs.

'Right, thank you, Philip.' Rachel started to climb the

stairs with Philip close behind her. 'Which bedroom?' she asked as she reached the landing.

'Oh, that one.' He pointed to a room at the back of the house whose door stood ajar. Rachel tapped on the door, walked into the room and instantly knew there was something wrong. She had been expecting the main bedroom, with Julie in a double bed. Instead, she found herself in a small narrow room, little more than a box room. There was a single bed in the room but it was empty. There was no sign of Julie, but most disturbing of all to Rachel was the fact that the wall facing her was covered with photographs of herself.

For one instant she was struck dumb as she gazed at the wall. The photographs were mostly old ones—her as a child in the garden of Ashton House, as a teenager at some party or other—but there were others, more recent ones, which had been enlarged, showing her at the Michaelmas Fair, with Georgie, on the dodgems and receiving her raffle prize. Then her brain leapt into gear and she rounded on Philip, who was standing very close behind her, blocking the doorway. 'What's going on, Philip?' she said, surprised at how calm her voice sounded. 'Where's Julie?'

'Julie isn't here,' he said, and his words sent a chill down Rachel's spine. 'It's just you and me now, Rachel.'

'I don't understand,' she said, her voice still calm in spite of the fact that her heart was beating rapidly and her mouth felt quite dry. 'You said Julie was ill…'

'That was the only way I knew to get you here,' he said, his tone matter-of-fact.

'So where is she?' As she spoke Rachel felt the hairs at the back of her neck begin to prickle.

He didn't answer, instead leaning forward to study his photograph collection more intently.

'Philip?' Rachel repeated urgently. 'Where is Julie?'

'She's left me,' he said at last.

'Left you?' Rachel frowned, surprised in spite of her fear.

'She's gone back to her mother,' he said. His voice was dull, flat and expressionless.

'But why?' Rachel demanded. 'I don't understand. I thought you two were happy. You were trying for a family. I thought…'

'We were,' he said in the same flat monotone, 'sort of, but then you came back, Rachel, and everything changed.'

She stared at him. 'You're saying that my coming back to Westhampstead changed things between you and Julie?'

'Of course it did.' He spoke scornfully, as if it should have been obvious.

'Well, I'm sorry, Philip,' she said, 'but I really don't see why.'

'Don't you?' He stared at her, and now his eyes with their sandy lashes seemed to bore into her. 'She always knew there was someone else,' he said, 'but she didn't know who, then yesterday she found these.' He indicated the photographs. 'She knows now that it's you, that it's always been you. She said she's had enough, can't stand it any more, so she's gone. But I don't care, Rachel, because that leaves me much more time to be able to see you.'

With a muffled exclamation Rachel tried to get past him but he was too fast for her, barring the door and her only escape route. 'Philip…' She took a deep breath. 'Please, let me go,' she said, striving to keep her voice as calm as possible and not give any indication of the panic she was feeling.

'I'm getting a bit tired of only being able to email you,' he went on, totally ignoring her request, 'and you didn't even bother to answer me.'

She stared at him. 'It was you,' she said, and the words seemed to stick in her throat.

'Of course it was me,' he said, kicking the door shut behind him. 'Who did you think it was—that Kowalski creep? I thought I'd put paid to him once before, but now he's back, sniffing around you again.'

At his words everything seemed to click into place but Rachel felt paralysed and utterly speechless, knowing now that she was probably dealing with a man with a deadly obsession that had haunted him for years.

'I love you,' he said. 'I've always loved you. We grew up together at Ashton House. We were always together, you and I.'

'We were children, Philip…' she protested.

'We were always meant to be together,' he argued, and there was an edge of anger in his voice now. 'If you hadn't started going out with Kowalski everything would have been all right, but then you went away and I didn't see you for years. I met Julie…she wanted to get married. I told her there was someone else, someone who I would always love, and she said it didn't matter, that she understood. But then you came back, Rachel, you came back for me. It's all meant to be, don't you see?' He took a step towards her, reaching out for her, and she backed away, putting up her hands to ward him off.

'Philip, don't do this,' she said desperately. 'Think about…your mother…'

'My mother liked you,' he said. 'She always said what a lovely daughter-in-law you would make.'

'But she wouldn't like this, Philip, you driving Julie

away and tricking me into coming here…she wouldn't like that at all…'

'I don't care,' he said. 'I've got you here now. This is all I've ever dreamed of, all I've ever wanted.' He moved forward and attempted to pull her into his arms. She twisted frantically to try to get away from him.

'We'll be happy, Rachel,' he said, 'just you and me, and later we could have a baby. I bet I could get *you* pregnant.'

That was the moment that Rachel lost her composure completely and screamed at the top of her voice. Philip tried to silence her, then the next moment all hell seemed to break loose as the door burst open and the room was suddenly full of people. Uniformed police officers were everywhere, Terry Payne was there, and Nick—Nick who pulled Rachel roughly into his arms and held her while two policemen restrained Philip. Terry arrested and cautioned him and he was led away, out of the room, down the stairs and into a waiting squad car.

'Oh, Nick.' Rachel leaned weakly against him, the tears pouring down her cheeks. 'Oh, thank God you came. I thought…I really thought…'

'Don't,' he said softly against her hair, 'not now. Later. Let's get you home now.'

'But how did you know?' It was much later and Rachel and Nick were at the house in Cathedral Close. Rachel had taken a hot shower while Nick had lit a fire to take the edge off the damp chill of the autumn evening and now, wrapped in a warm bathrobe, Rachel reached up and took the glass of brandy that Nick passed to her.

'I had an inkling,' he said, sitting beside her on the sofa and cradling his own glass of brandy in his hands. 'Not about the emails, of course, because I thought we had that tied up, but about the letter. I had found myself thinking that it had to have been written by someone who was around at the time, someone who knew you very well, well enough to forge your handwriting, and someone who also knew me, and all about our situation. I cast my mind right back to those days and for some reason I thought of Philip Newton.'

'You did?' She turned her head and looked at him in surprise. The only light in the room was that of the fire.

'Yes.' He nodded. 'He was always around, wasn't he? Whenever I came to Ashton House he was lurking around the garden or the drive.'

'Well, he did live there with his mother,' Rachel said slowly. 'They had a flat at the top of the house for all the years that Elsie Newton was our housekeeper.'

'So he would have known all the comings and goings in the house?'

'Well, yes, I suppose he would,' she admitted.

'And did you and he spend a lot of time together?'

'We used to play together as children,' she said, her forehead wrinkling as she tried to recall those days. 'He used to come to my birthday parties—that sort of thing. I think my mother felt sorry for him, what with his father going off and leaving them when Philip was only five.'

'Did you know he'd formed an attachment to you?' asked Nick.

Rachel frowned again. 'I suppose I was aware of it,' she admitted at last. 'He used to follow me around and once when we were about ten or eleven he said that one day we would get married. But then when I went away to school I guess I never thought any more about it. He did ask me out once, now that I think of it, and I...I turned him down.'

'Goodness knows what that did to him,' said Nick grimly. 'My guess is he didn't take rejection too well.'

Rachel took a sip of her brandy. 'Honestly, Nick,' she said after a moment, 'it never crossed my mind since coming back here that it was him…that he could be responsible…' She bit her lip and trailed off, staring into the fire as she relived those terrifying moments in Philip's house.

The only sound in the room was the crackling of a log that Nick had thrown onto the fire. 'How…how did you know where to find me?' asked Rachel at last, looking up at Nick.

'Well, like I say, I'd already had an inkling that he might have been responsible for writing that letter,' Nick admitted, 'then when I got your message about receiving another email I went straight to the medical centre. They told me you were out on an emergency. When I asked where you had gone they seemed reluctant to tell me— patient confidentiality and all that—but Bruce Mitchell overheard the conversation and he stepped in. As soon as I told him I feared you might be in danger, he told me that you'd been called to the Newtons' house. I knew then for certain that my hunch had been correct. I radioed in for back-up and the rest you know.'

'Oh, Nick.' She rested her head on his shoulder. 'If you hadn't come…'

'Don't,' he said firmly, slipping one arm around her and holding her tightly, 'don't even think about it.'

'What will happen to him?' asked Rachel after a moment.

'He's up before the magistrates tomorrow for stalking.'

'But he's sick. He needs help, Nick.'

'Yes, I know—I imagine there will be recommendations for psychiatric reports before it goes any further.'

'I feel sorry for Julie,' said Rachel after a moment. 'He said she knew he had a fixation with someone from the start but that she was prepared to accept the situation—then I came back to Westhampstead.' She paused. 'She didn't know it was me even then—to think we've been working together…' She shook her head.

'Did he say how she found out?' asked Nick.

'He said she found the photographs. She must have snapped, Nick. He said she'd left him and gone back to her mother. It must have been pretty spooky for her, finding all those photographs—there were dozens of them right back from when I was a child. Most of them had been blown right up…well, you know, you saw them. Oh, Nick, maybe I shouldn't have come back.' Her voice shook.

'Nonsense,' he said firmly. 'Of course you should have come back—the fact that Philip Newton chose to destroy his marriage by stalking you is no one's fault but his own. I rather suspect that Julie might have discovered his weird ways long before you came back. She may not have known it was you, but she must have realised that the man she was married to had some very odd habits.'

'He must have got my email address from Julie,' Rachel said slowly, then with a little start she said, 'Although, no, perhaps not. There was a time he came to the surgery with Julie and he would have been on his own in my consulting room while I was examining her— it would have been easy for him to look up my address on the computer. And on another occasion,' she added, as the memories flooded back, 'he was selling raffle tickets for the Michaelmas Fair—I can remember filling in all my details, including my address and phone number. He was clever, Nick, and very devious.'

'You're right.' He took another sip of his brandy. 'And going back all those years ago to that letter, he must have found samples of your handwriting around Ashton House, even an old envelope from a letter you'd sent home, and practised copying it until he had it so perfect that even I was fooled. He must also have travelled to London to post it so that the postmark would have been right.'

'And the flowers,' said Rachel. 'He must have heard that yellow roses were my favourite flowers when he was at Ashton House.'

'That's just the sort of thing someone like him would remember,' said Nick.

'And it was him sitting outside here late at night,' said Rachel with a shudder. 'I could only see a shadow sitting in the passenger's seat—at the time I thought the driver, whoever he was, was visiting someone in a house in the close. I realise now that it was because he would have been seen in the streetlight if he had been sitting on the other side. He saw you leave here that night, Nick...' She began to shake and gently he extricated the glass from her fingers and, setting it down on a low table beside the sofa, turned and gathered her into his arms.

'It's all right,' he said softly against her hair, 'it's all right, Rachel, really it is. The nightmare's over now. I'm here...'

He held her close for a long time as they sat there in the flickering light of the fire.

'To think I blamed my mother...' said Rachel at last, breaking the silence.

'You mustn't forget the fact that your mother didn't

like me,' protested Nick mildly, 'and she did tell you that I was seeing someone else when I wasn't.'

'And Tommy—poor Tommy Page. I even blamed him...' Rachel shook her head in distress. 'I still think it might have been better for everyone if I'd never come back to Westhampstead,' she added shakily.

'Do you know what I think?' said Nick, tilting her chin and looking deeply into her eyes. 'I think you shouldn't have gone away in the first place. I think we should have stayed together all those years ago then no one and nothing would have ever come between us.'

'So are you saying that we've had our chance, that it's too late for us now?' she said. Lifting her hand with one finger she gently traced a line down his face and across his lips.

'I'm not saying anything of the sort,' he replied. Catching her hand with one of his own, he held it, imprisoning it against his face. 'What I am saying is that I believe we're being given a second chance—that this is our time now. We were meant to be, Rachel, you know that as well as I do.'

'Yes,' she whispered, 'I know.'

'So is that how it is going to be from now on? You and me together against the world?'

'Yes, but with one exception.'

'Which is?'

'A lot of the time it will be you, me and Lucy,' she said.

'Bless you for that,' he murmured, and quite suddenly his voice was unexpectedly husky. Then his arms tightened around her again. 'I love you, Rachel,' he said. 'I've always loved you.'

'I love you, too,' she replied, and as the log suddenly spluttered and fell apart, sending sparks shooting up the chimney, with a deep sigh of satisfaction she slid her arms around his neck and drew his face towards her own, knowing as she did so with a sudden deep certainty that from that moment onwards everything really was going to be all right.

THE DOCTOR'S TENDER SECRET by *Kate Hardy*

(London City General)

On the hectic paediatrics ward of London City General, love just isn't running smoothly for Dr Brad Hutton and Dr Zoe Kennedy. They may be instantly smitten with each other once again, but the secrets they have kept locked away make their future together uncertain. For Brad, the solution lies in putting his past behind him. But Zoe's secret goes a lot deeper…

AIRBORNE EMERGENCY by *Olivia Gates*

(Air Rescue)

Surgeon Cassandra St James couldn't wait to join the Global Aid Organisation's flying Jet Hospital – until she encountered mission leader Vidal Santiago. What was this millionaire plastic surgeon – the man she loved and loathed – doing on a humanitarian mission? Had she misjudged him? And could she control the unwanted passion that flared between them?

OUTBACK DOCTOR IN DANGER by *Emily Forbes*

When an explosion rocks a peaceful Outback town, flying doctor Matt Zeller is on hand to help. He hasn't been emotionally close to anyone for years, and has dedicated himself to his work – then he meets Nurse Steffi Harrison at the scene. She's due to stay in town for just a few weeks – but after knowing her for mere moments Matt knows he wants her to stay!

On sale 7th January 2005

M3/98

Published 17th December 2004

TESS GERRITSEN

BARBARA DELINSKY

Two emotionally compelling novels by international
bestselling authors in one special volume

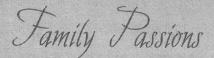

Family Passions

No. 1 *New York Times* bestselling author

NORA ROBERTS

presents two classic novels about the walls people build around their hearts and how to break them down...

Love by Design

Available from 21st January 2005

On sale 7th January 2005

FREE!

4 Books
and a surprise gift!

We would like to take this opportunity to thank you for reading this Mills & Boon® book by offering you the chance to take FOUR more specially selected titles from the Medical Romance™ series absolutely FREE! We're also making this offer to introduce you to the benefits of the Reader Service™—

- ★ **FREE home delivery**
- ★ **FREE gifts and competitions**
- ★ **FREE monthly Newsletter**
- ★ **Exclusive Reader Service offers**
- ★ **Books available before they're in the shops**

Accepting these FREE books and gift places you under no obligation to buy. you may cancel at any time. even after receiving your free shipment. Simply complete your details below and return the entire page to the address below. You don't even need a stamp!

YES! Please send me 4 free Medical Romance books and a surprise gift. I understand that unless you hear from me. I will receive 6 superb new titles every month for just £2.69 each, postage and packing free. I am under no obligation to purchase any books and may cancel my subscription at any time. The free books and gift will be mine to keep in any case.

M4ZEF

Ms/Mrs/Miss/Mr ....Initials ....

BLOCK CAPITALS PLEASE

Surname ....

Address ....

....

....Postcode ....

Send this whole page to:
UK: FREEPOST CN81, Croydon, CR9 3WZ